"Get off me, Justin!" Stacey said fiercely, as the taxi gave a lurch and Justin's muscular body was thrown forcefully on top of her.

Justin's cheek grazed the soft skin of Stacey's bare shoulder and he raised his head. Their eyes met and held. For a long moment, neither spoke or moved or breathed.

Slowly, but of their own volition, Stacey's fingers slid from Justin's neck to weave through his raven-black hair. She became aware of his legs pressed against her own, the beat of his heart against her chest.

"Stacey." She heard his voice from far away and puzzled at the tone. It was a tortured plea of urgency and longing which she would never in a thousand years have associated with the icily controlled Justin Marks.

Then she saw his head descend toward her, and her lips parted in anticipation. It did not seem the least bit strange to be lying in a taxicab under the powerful body of the man she had teased and tormented and professed to loathe for the past ten years. . . .

WHAT ARE *LOVESWEPT* ROMANCES?

They are stories of true romance and touching emotion. We believe those two very important ingredients are constants in our highly sensual and very believable stories in the *LOVESWEPT* line. Our goal is to give you, the reader, stories of consistently high quality that may sometimes make you laugh, sometimes make you cry, but are always fresh and creative and contain many delightful surprises within their pages.

Most romance fans read an enormous number of books. Those they truly love, they keep. Others may be traded with friends and soon forgotten. We hope that each *LOVESWEPT* romance will be a treasure—a "keeper." We will always try to publish

LOVE STORIES YOU'LL NEVER FORGET
BY AUTHORS YOU'LL ALWAYS REMEMBER

The Editors

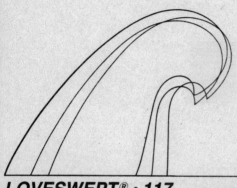

LOVESWEPT® • 117

Barbara Boswell
Landslide Victory

 BANTAM BOOKS
TORONTO • NEW YORK • LONDON • SYDNEY • AUCKLAND

LANDSLIDE VICTORY

A Bantam Book / November 1985

LOVESWEPT® *and the wave device are registered
trademarks of Bantam Books, Inc. Registered in U.S. Patent
and Trademark Office and elsewhere.*

ISBN 0-553-21732-1

Published simultaneously in the United States and Canada

---

*Bantam Books are published by Bantam Books, Inc. Its
trademark, consisting of the words "Bantam Books" and
the portrayal of a rooster, is Registered in U.S. Patent and
Trademark Office and in other countries. Marca Registrada.
Bantam Books, Inc., 666 Fifth Avenue, New York, New
York 10103.*

PRINTED IN THE UNITED STATES OF AMERICA

O   0 9 8 7 6 5 4 3 2 1

One

Stacey Lipton confirmed her pregnancy at home, using a pregnancy testing kit purchased in a drugstore. She followed the directions to the letter; the positive reading was not a mistake. She was pregnant. And unmarried. And in just a few hours her father, Bradford Lipton, the senior senator from Nebraska, was scheduled to announce his candidacy for the office of president of the United States.

She'd known for a long time, of course. Her calculations placed her in the middle of her third month, and she'd had all the signs and symptoms for weeks. The missed periods, the morning sickness, the fatigue. She'd had no significant weight gain yet, but her breasts were fuller and uncomfortably tender, and she could no longer wear certain clothes because her waistline had begun to thicken.

Over the months she'd progressed from full-blown panic to a sort of fearful resignation, but today was the first time she'd sought irrefutable proof of her condition. And now she had it. Her father—the arch-conservative, the traditional, staunch, back-to-old-fashioned-morals-and-family candidate—would become a grandfather again in six months via his unmarried daughter.

His unmarried twenty-five-year-old daughter,

who should have known better, who should have been more careful. Who'd lost her head one night last August with a man she'd disliked intensely for ten years—Justin Marks, her father's longtime administrative assistant and, as of today, his national campaign manager. Justin Marks, a man whose disapproval of Bradford Lipton's daughter equaled his admiration of the senator.

A rush of heat surged through her as unwelcome memories of that hot August night tumbled crazily through her mind. The Rotary Club—or was it the Kiwanis? Stacey couldn't remember— had awarded her father their special Man-of-the-Year award. As her mother was in Nebraska for a women's club dinner, Stacey had been sent along with her father instead. And of course, Justin Marks, the indispensable right-hand man, the brilliant political strategist of the Lipton camp, had come to the awards dinner too. . . .

While her father waited in his car, Justin had come to the door of her apartment to collect her. Tall at six-foot-two, he'd seemed even taller in his black tuxedo, and his piercing black eyes had assessed Stacey in her red-silk cocktail dress with unconcealed censure. "You're not planning to wear *that*?"

She'd known he wouldn't approve when she'd selected the dress. It was too red, the back was too low-cut, the neckline too deeply scooped. "Yes, I am planning to wear *this*," she replied with acid sweetness. "Let me guess, you don't approve of bare arms?"

"You're not wearing anything under it," he said, his teeth clenched. "Stacey, these are solid family men. You can't wear that dress! It's too—too—" He coughed.

"Too what, Justin?" she asked, grinning.

Unnerving Justin Marks was always one of her favorite pastimes.

"Wear something else, Stacey," he ordered flatly.

"What do you suggest I wear, Justin?" she baited him. She liked to bait him almost as much as she enjoyed unnerving him.

"What about that pretty white dress of yours?" Justin *always* took the bait. "The one with the ruffles and long sleeves and blue ribbons?"

"You're describing my high-school graduation dress." Her good humor was beginning to evaporate. What nerve the man had, telling her to change her dress! Stacey glowered at him as he stood before her, so tall and hard and lean, with those intense black eyes of his that always seemed to be watching her. "I'm not changing my dress, Justin." She made it a point to refuse to obey all of his obnoxious decrees. "This one is perfectly fine for tonight."

"It isn't, Stacey. You ought to look like the demure daughter of a senator, not—not like a flashy Las Vegas show girl."

That did it! "I don't look like a showgirl simply because I like a little color and style, Justin Marks!" She was furious with him, which was par for the course in their relationship. Her gaze traveled over the sharp, hawklike features of his face, his thick, blue-black hair, cut conservatively short, of course, and her hostility mounted. "You look like—like an undertaker in that black monkey suit!" He did, too, she assured herself. He looked drab and depressingly somber and big and dark and . . . At that point, Stacey stopped thinking and swept grandly from her apartment. Justin Marks had no choice but to follow.

The Man-of-the-Year award had been presented to Bradford Lipton and he'd given a rousing, presidential-sounding speech. And then came the party afterward. Stacey groaned at the memory. What a party! The "solid family men" —Elks? Lions? Would she ever remember—kept the liquor flowing in an awesome, never-ending stream. Every time Stacey took a sip of her drink, her glass was refilled to the brim. She'd noted with malicious amusement that Justin Marks, normally an abstemious teetotaler, had met the same fate. A martini was literally forced on him and she watched him slowly sip the drink until his glass was half empty.

"Oh, Justin, your drink needs freshening!" she remarked ingenuously—and within careful earshot of a hospitable member of the Moose—Optimists? Whatever.

"Why, it sure does!" exclaimed the jovial club member, and immediately he splashed straight gin into Justin's glass.

"This really isn't necessary," Justin said with forced amiability, but his icy, black gaze was fixed on Stacey.

"Sure, it is. We all want to have a good time, don't we, boy?" The man slapped Justin on the back. "No stiffs allowed in here tonight."

"No stiffs allowed, boy," Stacey echoed gleefully. She felt nothing but merriment at Justin's plight. He didn't dare offend this aggressive group of potential supporters of his candidate. And it was a particular delight to call the thirty-nine-year-old Justin Marks "boy". How many years had she had to endure "little girl" from him?

During the long evening, everyone kept proposing toasts to her father, and the glasses inevitably would be refilled. By the end of the evening, Senator Lipton was proclaimed a lifelong honorary member of the club and had garnered a roomful of votes.

And by the end of the evening, Stacey was feeling

an irrepressible gaiety. These club men were really fun people, she decided, viewing the scene through a hazy warmth. When a seventy-eight-year-old veteran asked her to Charleston with him, she laughingly accepted. Bradford Lipton smiled indulgently and suggested that Justin see Stacey home, as he was leaving now himself.

Justin Marks took his assignments very seriously. At midnight, he told Stacey that she was leaving and Stacey, in the middle of a rousing rendition of "We Could Make Believe" with a chorus of aging baritones, refused to go. Amid cheers and whistles, Justin scooped her up in his arms and carried her out of the hall. For a moment, Stacey was too stunned to speak. Justin Marks *never* created a scene. He was the epitome of stuffed-shirt propriety. And then a thought occurred to her.

"Are you drunk, Justin?" she said softly, tauntingly. "Did you make one toast too many?" It was so strange to be in his arms, she thought. She felt the strength in his whipcord muscles, felt the warmth of his big hands under her thighs. Her head seemed to rest naturally against his chest, which was broad and hard and peculiarly inviting. She gazed limpidly into his eyes and noted that his pupils seemed to have merged with the irises, making them blacker than she'd ever seen them. He had long, thick lashes—she'd never noticed just how long and thick they actually were. But then, she'd never been this close to him before.

"I am *not* drunk," was his severe reply.

"Not even a little?" she teased in a singsong voice.

"Shut up, Stacey," he said through clenched teeth. His mouth was set in a tight, straight line, and Stacey playfully traced the curve of his lips with her dark red-polished fingernail.

"Can you walk a straight line, Justin?" She

couldn't seem to resist the impulse to continue teasing him. He had a beautifully shaped mouth, she observed with bemused detachment. It was usually clamped into a forbidding, stern line and she'd never noticed the fine shape before. But she did now. He really did have a beautiful mouth.

"Quit it, Stacey!" But his voice wasn't as steady as it usually was when he was issuing one of his imperious edicts.

"Quit it, Stacey. Shut up, Stacey," she said, unsuccessfully imitating his deep tones. Then she laughed. "No, Justin. I'm not going to quit it and I'm not going to shut up. And you can't make me!" she added merrily.

She felt him draw in a deep breath and knew he was furious. Nothing new there. He was always furious with her for one reason or another, it seemed. Since he'd first joined her father's staff as AA ten years ago, Justin Marks had consistently disapproved of the senator's daughter. She knew he disliked her and the feeling was extraordinarily mutual.

There was a taxi waiting in front of the hall, and Justin carried her to it. Whether the driver was waiting for someone else or not, Justin Marks simply commandeered the cab. He had an authoritative air that made headwaiters seat him at their best tables and congressional staffers run to do his bidding. "Insufferably domineering," Stacey had called him on more than one occasion. Obnoxious. Arrogant. Dictatorial. In her opinion, he was all of these and worse.

The driver agreed to take them to Stacey's Northwest Washington apartment and he leaned over the seat to open the door from the inside. Justin caught the door and attempted to deposit Stacey in the backseat.

And then he tripped. Whether he stumbled over

the curb or lost his footing because of one too many martinis, neither of them would ever know. He pitched forward and Stacey's arms automatically tightened around his neck as they fell. A dizzying, disorienting second later, she was on her back on the seat of the taxi with Justin Marks on top of her. Her arms were wrapped around his neck and her legs were tangled with his. The spicy scent of his after-shave mixed with her jasmine-floral cologne and wafted into their nostrils as they simultaneously inhaled.

"Get off me, you oaf!" Stacey said.

"Damn!" Justin said.

Someone slammed the door shut and the taxi lurched forward. Justin's cheek grazed the soft skin of Stacey's bare shoulder and he raised his head. Their eyes met and held. For a long moment, neither spoke or moved or even breathed.

Stacey saw herself reflected in his dark, dark eyes. Her chin-length nut-brown hair was splayed around her head on the seat, her heavy bangs covering her forehead. Her wide set, tawny, brown eyes gazed up at him, slightly dazed. She had a small snub nose with a smattering of freckles across it, a firm little chin, and a wide, generous mouth. When she smiled, which she did often, she'd been told she "radiated that Lipton family charm."

Justin lay heavily upon her, yet surprisingly his weight no longer felt oppressive. Her body seemed to have accustomed itself to him, absorbing the impact and adjusting to the hard warmth. They continued to stare at each other, and, of their own volition, Stacey's fingers slid from his neck to the short thickness of his raven-black hair. She became aware of his leg trapped between her own, of her breasts pressed tightly against the hard breadth of his chest.

"Stacey." She heard his voice from far away and puzzled at his tone. It was a tortured plea of urgency and longing that she would have never in a thousand years associated with the icily controlled Justin Marks.

With a kind of fatalistic submission, she saw his head descend toward her, and her lips parted in anticipation. It did not seem the least bit strange to be lying in a taxicab under the powerful body of the man she had teased and tormented and professed to loathe for the past ten years. . . .

"Stace?" There was a light tap on the bathroom door and Stacey was reluctantly drawn back into the present. "May I come in?" Brynn Cassidy didn't wait for a response. She entered the bathroom, took one look at Stacey, and gulped. "The test was . . . positive?"

Stacey nodded. "I knew it would be, Brynn."

"I wish you'd told me sooner." Brynn's usually merry face was grave. "When I think of you keeping it to yourself all this time . . ." Her voice trailed off sadly.

"I guess I was denying it to myself, Brynn. Like the proverbial ostrich in the sand—if I didn't acknowledge it, it didn't exist." Stacey sighed deeply. "But Dad's announcement today finally galvanized me into action."

"Oh, Stacey!" Brynn sat down beside her on the rim of the bathtub. "Oh, Stacey!" her usually articulate and verbal friend murmured again.

Stacey looked at Brynn's downcast green eyes, saw her auburn ponytail droop as she lowered her head, and knew that Brynn was suffering for her. "You're the first and only person I've told, Brynnie." Stacey shredded a wad of tissues with nervous fingers. It hadn't been too hard, telling Brynn. They'd been friends since junior high school, had roomed together in college, and had shared this apartment for the past four and a half years. To Stacey, Brynn was the sister she'd never had, and she trusted her implicitly. It had been Brynn who'd bought the pregnancy-testing kit at the drugstore. Senator Lipton's daughter didn't dare make such a purchase herself, not with the media spotlight that surrounded the Lipton family these days.

"Stace?" Brynn paused and swallowed. "Do you mind if I ask who the father is?"

Stacey could almost read her friend's mind. Brynn knew that Stacey hadn't been seriously involved with anyone for a long, long time. And she knew Stacey's feelings about casual sex. Senator Lipton's daughter didn't indulge in it and Stacey Lipton herself found it repugnant. So who? . . . and how? . . .

"Brynn, it's Justin Marks," Stacey blurted out, for there was no easy way to say it.

Had Stacey confessed that the father was the premier of the Soviet Union, Brynn couldn't have looked more stunned. "Justin Marks!" She gasped and jerked backward, her astonishment propelling her off the rim and into the empty bathtub.

Stacey looked at Brynn sprawled in the tub, her jeans-clad legs half over the rim, and burst into laughter. Seconds later she was crying, her tears flowing so fast she was choking on them, her shoulders shaking with sobs.

Brynn scrambled out of the tub and put her arms around Stacey. "Don't cry, Stace. We'll—we'll work it out somehow." She sounded as hopeless as Stacey felt. "When did it happen?"

"August." Stacey closed her eyes. "Remember those two weeks you spent at your brother's place in New Hampshire?"

"Oh, Lord," breathed Brynn. "I remember."

Stacey was remembering too. She was lying in

the backseat of the taxi, her arms wrapped tightly around Justin as he lay on top of her. The impact of his mouth upon hers catapulted her into stunning, sensual shock. Never had she felt this shattering sexuality, this explosive desire. His tongue surged into her mouth and she met it with her own, boldly rubbing and challenging. His mouth was hot and hard and demanding, and he kissed her in a way that she'd never been kissed before. Deeper, more intimate, primitively possessive. As if she belonged to him and he was staking his claim at last.

His kiss displayed the masculine assurance that Justin Marks projected in all aspects of his life, but suddenly Stacey didn't find him unbearably high-handed. Instead of being inspired to challenge him, to rail against him, some feminine instinct within her welcomed him with sweet submission. She gloried in his strength and power. She clung to him, moving sensuously beneath him and kissing him back with a possessive ardor that equaled his own.

"Stacey, Stacey." He lifted his mouth from hers and whispered her name with an urgency that thrilled her. Sometimes he uttered, "Stacey!" in a disapproving reprimand; sometimes he snapped, "Stacey!" in an infuriating command. She responded to both with taunts or anger. But the passion and hunger in his voice now released a wild and totally unexpected response within her. A tidal wave of feelings overwhelmed her.

Her breasts were swollen and her nipples were taut and aching. She caught his hand and placed it firmly against her burgeoning softness. His thumb traced the outline of one hard bud through the red silk, back and forth, methodically, slowly, until she moaned and arched upward in frustrated excitement. She wanted to feel his mouth upon her, and her own desire shocked her.

Justin laughed softly, triumphantly, against her ear. "I'm glad you didn't listen to me tonight, Stacey. I'm glad you didn't wear a bra."

Was she hallucinating? she wondered, bemused. His suggestive remark and his sexy laughter stunned her. And excited her too. The everyday Justin Marks didn't laugh—even a smile seemed to be an almost insurmountable effort for him. And the everyday Justin Marks would never admit that he was glad the senator's daughter hadn't worn a bra! Nor would the everyday Justin nibble enticingly on her earlobe or taste her skin with his tongue or cup her breast in his big hand and fondle her possessively.

But this was no hallucination. He felt big and strong and undeniably real as he lay on top of her. Stacey twisted restlessly beneath him and he inserted his thigh between her legs. When he began to apply a firm, erotic pressure, her hips moved against him with a responding sensual rhythm. Her dress was around her hips and he stroked the smooth expanse of her nylon-clad thigh with his long fingers.

She felt helpless, surrounded and possessed by him, and she burned with a passionate excitement she had never before experienced. She wanted him to be masterful, she wanted to cede all control and envelope him within her. It made no sense, for she was fiercely independent and zealously challenged all of his attempts to order her around, but she was beyond thinking rationally. She seemed driven by a force that urged her to give everything to the man in her arms.

Their mouths merged again and Stacey drank in the taste of him, her senses reeling. She had no recollection of how they ever got out of the taxi, but she did remember being held high in his arms as he fumbled with her key in the lock of her apartment door.

"Brynn's not here," she said, pressing urgent little kisses along the hard, tanned column of his neck. "Stay with me, Justin."

He smiled down at her—a real smile, for perhaps the first time in the entire decade of their stormy acquaintance—and murmured softly, "Yes, darling, I'll stay with you."

Darling! Who would have thought that the sober, intensely serious, and totally dedicated-to-her-father's-political-future Justin Marks even *knew* the word *darling*?

In her dreamy, passion-induced haze, Stacey decided she was in love. It seemed as if Justin had been destined all along to become her lover, and she had finally recognized and accepted her destiny. All that tension between them all these years had been a carefully fought sexual tension. She knew that now. She hadn't wanted to admit her attraction for her father's forceful administrative assistant and he hadn't dared to make a claim on the senator's rebellious—and for a long time, much too young—daughter. But tonight they had both surrendered to their destiny and it was so natural, so very right.

She lost both her red high-heeled sandals on the way to the bedroom. Justin carried her to her bedroom with unerring accuracy. "How did you know which room was mine?" she asked languidly, threading her fingers through the springy thickness of his hair. He'd certainly never been in her bedroom before.

"By the Lipton family photograph on your dresser," he said, his black eyes hot and intense. "I have the same picture on the desk in my office."

"You do?" She had never been inside his office,

although it was within the complex of Senator Lipton's suite in the Senate Office Building on Capitol Hill. Even in her present unclear state of mind, it struck her as odd that he kept a photograph of the Lipton family on his desk. The picture had been taken five years before and all the family members were in it, except her brother Spence's little girls, who hadn't been born then.

"Why don't you keep a picture of *your* family on your desk?" she asked as he laid her down on the bed. She knew he wasn't married, of course. What woman in her right mind would marry a robotic tyrant like him? Stacey had often exclaimed to Brynn. But surely he had a mother or sister or some nieces and nephews to display?

"I don't have a family," he replied, lowering the zipper on her dress. He slipped the red silk from her shoulders, exposing her small, pink-tipped breasts. Her nipples stood out, tight and hard, and Justin was unable to resist touching them.

"Kiss me there, Justin," Stacey whispered, all inhibitions gone. She clasped his head to her breast and lovingly stroked his hair.

His mouth fastened over one aching nipple and he laved it with his tongue, arousing it even more, and making her squirm with sensual pleasure. When he began to suck erotically, she moaned and cried out his name.

"You're very sensitive there," he said with masculine satisfaction. "And so sweetly responsive, Stacey."

Her eyes were closed, but she smiled at the approval in his voice. She had pleased him, and at this moment, pleasing Justin Marks was the most important thing in her world.

"Your breasts are beautiful," he said huskily. "Round and firm and high. I wanted to see them like this, bare and swollen, just for me. I've always been able to tell when you were wearing a bra, and when you weren't I wanted to do this. . . ." Both his hands claimed her breasts and cupped and fondled and caressed.

Stacey whimpered her pleasure. She was swimming in a sea of sensuous delight and his every word and action swept her farther away. She felt him slip her dress and pantyhose past her hips and lifted obligingly so he could remove it. He tossed them to the floor and stared at her with passion-glazed eyes. She was wearing only her red bikini panties, and she flexed her knee and gave him a sexy, languorous smile.

"Tell me you want me, Justin," she murmured, dizzy with a thrilling sense of feminine power. No man had ever looked at her with such adoration, such undisguised need. Justin Marks was completely in her power. He was hers, all hers, and she watched him with possessive golden-brown eyes.

"Oh, Stacey, I want you so." He was fumbling with the small buttons on his starched white shirt. Stacey sat up to help him and proved just as shakily uncoordinated as he.

"Too bad it doesn't have a zipper," she lamented as they both struggled awkwardly with the difficult buttons.

"A dress shirt with a zipper? Sounds like something your brother Sterne would wear—unzipped to his navel, of course." Justin laughed at his own imagery, and it was a wonderful sound. Had she ever really heard him laugh before? she wondered. He was always so tense and on edge around her. She joined in his laughter, warmth surging through her. . . .

"When I think back on it, Stacey said dully to Brynn, "I can hardly believe it really happened." It was painful to return to the reality of the gray

November day. "We laughed and joked together. We teased each other. . . ."

"Justin Marks laughing and joking? That *is* hard to fathom, all right. I don't think I've ever seen the man crack a smile, Stace."

"And then"—Stacey swallowed hard—"we stopped laughing."

Her thoughts compulsively returned to that fateful August night. She'd helped Justin undress, right down to his white cotton briefs. Her eyes had been riveted to his long, hard frame. She'd never realized that he was so powerfully built. The charcoal-gray suits he wore so relentlessly called no attention to his muscular physique. A shiver of desire tingled through her.

Justin unselfconsciously removed his briefs and sat down on the bed. Stacey was drawn to him like a moth toward the light. She scrambled onto his lap and laid her head against the wiry dark hair covering his chest. His big arms enfolded her and he held her tightly for a long moment. And then his hands began to move.

He caressed her hips and thighs with long, slow strokes and she felt his lips brush the top of her head. She twined her arms around his neck and raised her face to his. His mouth closed over hers in a hungrily passionate kiss. "Oh, Justin," she sighed as he broke the kiss to stroke away the wispy red satin and lace from her body.

His hand slipped between her thighs to touch her intimately, possessively. "So silky and soft," he murmured. "My sweet Stacey." He kissed her deeply while he probed her tight warmth.

"Oh, Justin!" She was hot and moist to his touch. "Oh, Justin, please. Please!" She wanted him so much that she unabashedly pleaded with him for more.

"Stacey, you're on fire for me," he said with pure

masculine delight. "You want me, darling. You really need me."

"Oh, yes, Justin." She had to tell him just how much. "I've never felt this way before. I want you so much. I need you, Justin. I'm burning for you!"

"And I need you, Stacey." He kissed her again as he lowered her gently back onto the mattress. "Stacey." His voice seemed to come from far away. "My darling, my own."

She felt cherished and safe and loved. Opening herself to him, Stacey gave herself to Justin Marks with all the love and passion she possessed. And he took her with a breathtaking mastery. Clinging to him, she called his name as she was carried into a rapturous pleasure world she'd never dreamed existed. She was a part of him and she never wanted to be separate from him again. When she feel into a deep, dreamless sleep, Stacey was still holding her lover in her arms.

Justin roused her twice during that long, passionate night, and they made love again and again with all the fervor and tenderness and fire of before. Stacey remembered all of it with the oddly unreal quality of a dream. But it wasn't until she'd awakened late the next morning that the nightmare had begun. . . .

"I woke up next to him in my bed," Stacey confided haltingly to Brynn. "And I sort of—uh—screamed. That woke *him* up."

"Did he scream too?" Brynn asked dryly.

"I think he probably wanted to." Stacey swallowed, remembering. "He looked at me and at the bed and—and his face . . ." She didn't want to remember the look on his face when she'd stared at him and shrieked in recalled horror. She had run from the bedroom screaming, "What have I done?" Justin had called her name and followed her. "I locked myself in the bathroom," she said to Brynn, and "hollered at him to go away. I—I was so upset, Brynn."

"Understandably," she said soothingly.

"I'd never done anything like that before in my life!"

"I know, Stace."

"I'm an adult, Brynn." Stacey's voice rose. "A supposedly responsible, independent woman of twenty-five. I've never been reckless or careless, but that night—Brynnie, I never gave one thought to precautions of any kind."

"Who could have predicted what happened, Stacey?" Brynn said, attempting to comfort her. "You went to a testimonial dinner with your father and the unapproachable Justin Marks. You could have no idea that you'd end the night in bed with the 'Man with the Iron Control.' " Her lips curved into a small, mirthless smile. "He must have been really carried away, too, Stace. I can hardly imagine the 'Man with the Computerized Memory' forgetting to be careful. I always thought Justin Marks had microchips instead of brain cells. At least we now know he's actually human."

"What am I going to do, Brynn?" Stacey felt a panicky chill. Her mouth was dry and she could hardly swallow. "Justin and I have assiduously avoided each other since that night. I think I've only seen him four or five times since then and always, *always* in a crowd."

"Your arrangement," asked Brynn, "or his?"

"M-mine."

Brynn looked thoughtful. "How did you manage to get him out of the apartment that morning? You said you locked yourself in the bathroom and screamed for him to go away. Did he?"

"Not at first. He pounded on the door and kept telling me to calm down."

"Using his General-Patton-ordering-the-troopsto-advance tone?" guessed Brynn. "Or his prison-warden-commanding-the-chain-gang voice?"

"A combination of both, I think." But that was in the end, when she wouldn't stop crying and yelling and refused to let him in. In the beginning, he'd pleaded and coaxed her, his voice more gentle and tender than she'd ever heard. Stacey gave her head a shake, as if to clear it. She must've remembered it wrong; her memory was playing tricks on her. She couldn't accept Justin Marks as a soothing source of comfort. He'd been the enemy for too long!

"Justin told me I was hysterical and I guess I was a bit irrational," she said. "I just kept screaming at him to go away. I didn't want to see him or talk to him. I don't know why. Finally he left and I cried all day."

"Did he make any other attempts to contact you afterward?"

"He called me and I hung up on him. About a dozen times, maybe more. At last, I shouted into the phone that we both should forget that night ever happened, that it was a terrible mistake, and that I never wanted to be reminded of it." Stacey dried her eyes and blew her nose and splashed cold water on her flushed face. "But I've had a constant reminder, Brynn. I was terrified when I first began to suspect I was pregnant. It's taken me this long to face it and admit it to myself."

Brynn watched her with light green eyes narrowed with concern. "Do you know when the—uh—baby is due?"

"At the very end of April or the beginning of May." Stacey suddenly felt peculiarly faint. "Sometime after the New York and Pennsylvania primaries."

They exchanged bleak glances. "It would be bad politically if any senator's daughter was in this position," Stacey said, "disastrous for any presidential candidate's daughter, but for Senator Lipton's daughter . . ." She sat back down on the edge of the tub and held her head in her hands. "It's unthinkable. His ultraconservative supporters would turn on him and his less radical, but tradition-oriented supporters would feel betrayed. They'd see it as blatant promiscuity, a spurning of the old-fashioned values my father espouses. And can you imagine what the press would do with a story like this? They're lukewarm on my father to begin with. They'd have a field day!"

"Stacey." Brynn sat down beside her. "Have you given any thought to *not* having—er—it?" She spoke slowly, as if choosing her words very carefully.

Stacey shivered. "I've thought and thought about it, and I just can't *not* have it. Putting my father's candidacy aside, this is a *baby*, not an *it*. My baby."

"And Justin's," Brynn reminded her. "And I'm glad that you're not going to do . . . anything, Stace. I couldn't, either, if I was in your position."

"You mean in my condition," Stacey corrected her, and they smiled wanly at each other.

The telephone began to ring, but neither moved to answer it. On the fourteenth ring, Brynn sighed and slowly made her way to the kitchen phone. She was back a few seconds later, her face pale. "It's Justin Marks, Stacey. He wants to speak to you."

"We should have guessed it was him. Who else would let the phone ring twenty times without hanging up?" Justin Marks's tenacity and determination were ideal requisites for a senator's AA and for a national campaign manager, Stacey thought as she walked to the kitchen. She had heard Justin described by other political pols as ruthless, cunning, and instinctively correct in assessing weaknesses and strengths. Thankfully, Justin had no idea of what had resulted from that night of foolishly abandoned passion. But how long could she keep it a secret?

"Yes, Justin?" She spoke coolly into the telephone receiver, glad that her voice sounded steady. She'd certainly never felt less steady in her entire life!

"I wanted to remind you that your father will announce his candidacy in the Senate Caucus Room at four o'clock."

His officiously overbearing tone offended her. "I'm not likely to forget that," she replied crossly.

"And perhaps you'll dress appropriately for the occasion? Leave the leather miniskirt and green hair spray for some other time?"

From anyone else, Stacey would have known it was a joke and laughed accordingly. But Justin Marks didn't make jokes; he was always deadly serious. He actually believed she might show up in that sort of costume because she'd worn it several years before to a punk disco in New York City.

"That was a joke, Stacey, you're supposed to laugh," he astonished her by saying. She refused to believe it.

"You weren't joking, Justin, you're simply not taking any chances. And what do you suggest I wear today?" she asked with acid sweetness. "A charcoal-gray suit?"

Aside from his black tuxedo, she'd never seen him wear anything but a charcoal-gray suit, a white shirt, and a dark blue tie. Even in the summer, even at the beach! He'd actually come to the Liptons' beach house in Rehoboth in that getup. Stacey and Brynn used to speculate about the contents of his closet: there would be seven white shirts, seven charcoal-gray suits, and seven dark blue ties somberly hanging side by side. The image never failed to convulse them with laughter. Stacey's fingers tightened around the receiver. The father of her child wore a gray suit and black wing-tip shoes to the beach!

"I'm sure you'll dress to fit the occasion," Justin said, his voice cool and clipped. "Your mother is wearing a beige dress and pearls. Patty is wearing a green skirt with a green-and-blue blouse and a navy blazer."

"Patty isn't wearing overalls? How did you accomplish that?" Stacey asked curiously. She knew her brother Spencer's wife, Patty, unnerved Justin. Spence did too. The two of them were unconventional and unpredictable, the opposite of Justin and the senator. Patty and Spence lived on a small farm in Fredericksburg, Virginia, and their lifestyle was strictly back to nature. They worked the land, did their own canning, and cultivated herbs, which they brewed into tea. Both perpetually wore jeans or overalls. Spence had a full beard and a hoop earring in one ear and Patty had long, straight hair that hung below her hips. "Aging hippies" was the way Bradford Lipton described them, and he left Justin Marks to deal with them. He did so with restrained patience, although Stacey had seen him grit his teeth when they planned their infrequent campaign appearances by their astrology charts. Patty and Spence drove the incurably practical and conservative Justin Marks crazy.

"I took Patty shopping and chose her clothes myself," Justin said grimly. "She was going to wear those old patched jeans and a Save-the-Whales T-shirt."

"No wonder my father finds you indispensable," Stacey said. "No detail ever escapes you. You're so incredibly thorough."

"Why is it I don't think that's a compliment, coming from you?" Justin mused dryly. "This is an extremely important day, Stacey, perhaps the most historic in your father's career so far. Everything— and everyone—has to be perfect."

"And so you're calling all the black sheep in the Lipton family to make sure they conform to the conservative ideal of perfection?"

"And to remind you to be *on time*," he added.

The man was an obsessed robot, Stacey fumed. She had a brief flashback of them laughing together in bed and firmly put it from her mind. That night had been a bizarre aberration. The man wore a gray suit and white shirt every day of his life, for heaven's sake!

"You still haven't told me what you plan to wear today," Justin reminded her in that smoothly efficient tone of his.

"I thought I'd wear jeans and a Save-the-Whales T-shirt," she said.

"Stacey!"

"Well, somebody has to save the whales."

"Perhaps you'd rather I ask your mother to call you?" Justin asked, an edge of impatience creeping into his tone.

It was the last thing Stacey wanted. Her mother would have enough on her mind today without having to bother about her recalcitrant daughter. Stacey, like her three brothers, tried to protect her mother from whatever hassles she could. "Oh, give me a break, Justin, I was only kidding." The man had absolutely no sense of humor! "I'm wearing a teal wool dress, okay?"

"And may I safely assume you will not appear in those five-inch-heeled Lucite slides you once wore to the Senate Prayer Breakfast?"

"I was only seventeen at the time!" Stacey snapped. Brynn was right. Justin Marks did have a memory like a computer. He seemed to remember her every word and and action for the past ten years!

"I was only kidding, Stacey. It was a little joke."

She didn't want him to joke with her. For reasons that she didn't care to examine, she preferred to think of him as a humorless robot. "Suppose I wear those thick-heeled, black lace-up shoes like Grandmother Courtney wears? Will that be prim and proper enough for you?"

Justin ignored her remark. "Will your friend Brynn be coming with you today?"

"Of course. Brynn is like one of the family. Do you want to tell *her* to dress appropriately too?"

"I'll let you give her the message. Tell her to go directly to the Senate Caucus Room. There will be a seat reserved for her in the first row. You are to go to your father's office a half hour before the scheduled announcement. The whole family is going to proceed together to the Caucus Room.

"Another Justin Marks touch," Stacey said dryly. He recognized that an aura of togetherness would appeal to the senator's strongly pro-family supporters. Ironically, it never would have occurred to Bradford Lipton himself to gather his family together for a little private time before the historic moment. Justin Marks had been the one responsible for arranging such charades for the past ten years.

"Just be there, Stacey." His tone was dictatorial, the voice of the impeccably thorough campaign manager.

Stacey seethed, and then the words, "Yes, darling. I'll stay with you" echoed in her head. They were so clear that for one startling moment she thought he'd actually spoken them aloud. But, of course, he hadn't. It was her treacherous mind playing tricks on her again, plunging her into another of those queer flashbacks. She saw him poised above her in bed, his black eyes boring into her very soul. She drew in her breath sharply. In her passion-drugged state, she'd actually believed that she loved him!

Ha! The coldly sober Stacey forced herself to picture Justin as he was right now, as he always was, dressed in the conservative, dull suit, issuing orders to her in that authoritative manner of his while he thumbed through his Rolodex of detailed, coded cards. No one could love such a cold, emotionless automaton, she reminded herself.

A flash of anger made her burn. "Good-bye, Justin," she said crossly, and abruptly hung up.

Two

When people read in the papers about the gathering of the Lipton clan in Bradford Lipton's office, they would be led to believe that it was an extremely private time for the family to share their thoughts and emotions on this important occasion. The press release would say that Bradford Lipton had led his family in quiet prayer and poignant reminiscences.

When Stacey read the press release, composed by Justin Marks himself, she suggested that he take up fiction writing. The scene in Senator Lipton's office was not the serene, idyllic family portrait invented by Justin. It was a typical Lipton family gathering, with chaos, confusion, and tension being the order of the day.

Stacey dispatched Brynn to the Senate Caucus Room and arrived at her father's office ten minutes past the designated time. A number of close aides and staff members were waiting with Justin Marks in the large reception area of the office suite.

"You're late," Justin told her succinctly. He was tight-lipped and grim. Apparently, the rest of the family was late too.

His black eyes flicked over her mustard-colored knit dress. Actually, it was Brynn's dress, and the only dressy item in either of their wardrobes that fit Stacey properly. She'd tried on her teal wool dress only to find it unbearably constricting. None of her other dresses fit right either. Her breasts were too full for some, her waist too thick for others, and the soft, slight swell of her abdomen too evident in the rest.

Brynn's peach-toned complexion allowed her to wear such colors as mustard, but Stacey had looked at herself in the mirror and groaned. "This color makes me look sallow." Brynn had loyally disagreed, of course, but Stacey knew it was true. Mustard was definitely not the color for her.

Justin stared at her, frowning. "I thought you were going to wear a teal-blue wool dress. That color . . ." His voice trailed off.

"Makes me look sallow," Stacey finished for him. She was not going to allow him to be diplomatic. "Isn't that what you were about to say, Justin?"

"No," he protested.

"Yes, you were, and you're right. I do look sallow in this dress."

"I suppose I dare not ask why you wore a dress in a color that you know makes you look—er—sallow?"

Stacey scowled. "No, don't ask. Do you at least approve of my shoes, your excellency?" She was wearing plain black pumps with two-inch heels, boosting her height to five-foot-five, her mother's height without heels. Stacey had always longed for those extra inches. She considered five-three to be too short. Her brothers were tall, her father was tall. How did she happen to inherit short Grandmother Courtney's genes?

Justin stared at the black pumps and his lips quirked into a smile. "A nice compromise between the Lucite slides and Grandmother Courtney's lace-ups." He invited her to smile with him, and she nearly did. "Do you know this is the first time you've let me near enough to talk with you since August?" he asked bluntly, and Stacey felt her face flush with color. Trust Justin to seize the opportunity to be aggressively frank, she thought. He knew exactly how and when to catch a person off guard.

"I see my brother," she said with what she hoped sounded like frozen hauteur. "I'm going over to talk to him."

"Run away, little girl," Justin said, his voice so low only Stacey could hear. "But it won't be for much longer."

His words chilled her as she flew across the room to greet her oldest brother, Sterne. What had Justin meant?

"Stacey!" Sterne greeted her jovially. "Running away from the big enchilada, huh?" His eyes flicked toward Justin Marks. "What have you done now, Stace? Lost Dad the State of Iowa or something?"

"I was ten minutes late and I wore a dress that makes me look sallow. Can he lose Iowa over that?"

"Hey, I hear sallow is in these days." Sterne grinned at her. "No sign of Lucas, Spence, Patty, and the tribe yet. Think they'll make it on time?"

"Who knows?" Stacey gave a gleeful laugh. "Poor Justin. He probably has visions of them all tripping into the Caucus Room and interrupting Dad in the middle of the announcement." She gazed admiringly at her brother. "You really look terrific today, Sterne."

"Thanks, Stace." Sterne looked pleased. He was a thirty-two-year-old edition of his father, with the same handsome face, the same deep set dark blue eyes, and the same graceful six-foot-one height and carriage. But there were significant differences between the father and his eldest son. The senator had a thick shock of iron-gray hair, while Sterne's was light brown. And Sterne Lipton did not possess the intense ambition and dreams of power that motivated his father. Sterne owned a singles bar in Georgetown, and he reveled in his sybaritic, woman-chasing lifestyle. Justin Marks thoroughly disapproved of him, of course.

"I got a phone call today from *der Führer.*" Sterne cast an amused glance at Justin Marks. "He warned me *not* to show up in a black-silk blouson shirt unbuttoned to the waist and black jeans. And he said if I wore any gold chains or medallions he would use them to hang me."

Stacey giggled in spite of herself. "I guess you shouldn't have worn that particular outfit to Dad's Senate re-election victory party two years ago. Justin never got over it."

"Neither did Dad." For a moment Sterne's smile faded and his face became shuttered. Then he grinned at Stacey once more. "Well, here I am in a respectable blue suit, yellow shirt, and rep tie. What more can they ask for?"

"For Spence to shave his beard and remove the earring from his ear?" Stacey chuckled.

"Not a prayer of that. Hey, Lucas is here!" Sterne and Stacey walked over to greet their brother Lucas, the youngest of the family. Senator Lipton never failed to draw a laugh when he introduced his "baby" son, a twenty-year-old, six-foot-four, two-hundred-forty-pound defensive lineman on the University of Nebraska's football team.

"Lucas in a suit?" Stacey's eyes widened. "He must've had a phone call too!"

"Stacey!" Lucas extended his palms and Stacey gave him the obligatory double high five, his customary greeting to all. He and Sterne repeated the procedure. "Did you see me sack that wimpy Oklahoma quarterback last Saturday? They say he still isn't walking straight!" Lucas guffawed.

Justin Marks, standing nearby, winced at the

remark. When Lucas launched into an enthusiastic account of how he'd broken the nose of a Texas running back, Justin interrupted him. "Lucas, I don't want you to talk about your . . . maulings to any of the reporters today. This isn't the sports press, who might appreciate your triumphs. Today we're dealing with political reporters and analysts who may not approve of your dismembering your rivals."

"Oh, I get it!" Lucas nodded eagerly. "They're wimps, huh?"

Stacey could almost *hear* Justin mentally counting to ten before he walked away to speak to one of the speechwriters.

Spence and Patty Lipton arrived a few minutes later with their three small daughters, Sunshine, Melody, and Aurora, ages four, three, and two. All three little girls were dressed in pink smocked dresses, lacy white socks, and black patent-leather shoes. Stacey gaped at them in surprise. Her nieces always wore denim overalls and sneakers, like their parents. She couldn't recall ever seeing the children dressed in such typical little-girl fashion.

Her sister-in-law hugged and kissed Stacey. She always did. Patty hugged and kissed everyone in the family, although the Liptons were not given to physical displays of affection among themselves. "You look tired, Stacey," Patty said with her customary frankness. "Are you all right?"

"Of course," Stacey replied briskly, moving away from her. Patty probably had a sixth sense about pregnancy, living so close to the earth. She'd better keep her distance. "The children look sweet, Patty."

"Compliments of Justin Marks. He drove down to Fredericksburg one day last week and took us shopping. He picked out my outfit and the children's clothes too."

"Justin chose the children's clothes?" Stacey repeated incredulously.

"Right down to the fancy socks and party shoes, as he called them." Patty smiled. "He told me he wanted them to be dressed the way you were in that portrait of you in your dad's office."

Stacey knew the portrait, of course. It had been painted shortly after her fourth birthday, and she'd worn a pink smocked dress, pink hair ribbons, lacy socks, and black Mary Janes. Justin Marks had actually *looked* at that picture? she thought with amazement. And decided to outfit her nieces the same way?

"It's nice to know he approved of the way I dressed at one point in my life," she said dryly.

"He said you looked the way a little girl should look in that picture. Like a little princess." Patty grew momentarily serious. "Justin really isn't the ogre you Liptons make him out to be. He has an impossible role, you know. Your father uses him as a shield to hide behind from his family, and all of you take your resentment out on poor Justin."

"Poor Justin!" Spence said, and snorted. He had joined them in time to hear his wife's analysis. "You love everybody, Patty. We all know that Justin Marks is insufferable."

Spencer Lipton, thirty, was wearing a rather ill-fitting brown suit, and he hadn't shaved his bushy, reddish beard or removed the gold hoop earring. Still, he wasn't wearing his usual plaid shirt and coveralls, doubtless a credit to Justin's phone call. Stacey was certain of that.

"May I have your attention, please," Justin said. He held up his hand to quiet the group, taking charge as usual. For the first time, it occurred to Stacey that Justin Marks actually did stand in for the senator in an oddly paternalistic way. He was more involved in the details of the family members' lives than Bradford Lipton had ever been. It was a jarring thought.

"I want to outline the scenario around the senator's announcement," Justin continued, and was promptly interrupted by Sterne.

"What's to outline?" he said challengingly. "Dad makes his announcement and then we all split."

Justin threw him a quelling glance. "There is more to it than that. The whole family will be gathered behind the senator and in front of the press and the spectators. Please do not speak to the press at any time in the Caucus Room. We intend to have all questions addressed to Senator Lipton himself. *He* will sum up the family's feelings and reactions about—"

"How can Dad tell anyone about our feelings?" Spence interrupted. "He's never asked any of us how we felt about anything in our lives."

"Spence, this isn't an encounter group." Justin looked pained. "We're not here to discuss feelings, past, present, or future."

"Spence, you really can't expect Justin Marks to know anything about feelings, past, present, or future," Stacey added. "He doesn't have any. He operates on floppy discs instead of feelings."

"If I may proceed?" Justin looked directly at Stacey, his black eyes holding her golden-brown ones. She felt an odd tingling along her spine. It radiated to her abdomen, where it seemed to spark. It had been a long time since she'd stared into those deep, dark eyes. She felt suddenly hot and weak. Memories of lying naked in his arms, of feeling his big hands upon her, swept over her in a treacherous tide of emotion. She quickly lowered her eyes, her cheeks scarlet.

The rest of the family didn't seem to notice anything amiss. Patty linked her arm through Spence's and gave Justin her usual serene smile. "Please proceed, Justin."

He did. "All of you are to remain silent throughout the senator's announcement. He will make two small jokes and you are to laugh at both. When he extends his hand toward you in a sweeping gesture and makes reference to his supportive family, smile and—"

"Adoringly?" asked Stacey. The desire to irritate Justin was extraordinarily strong. She wanted to shake him out of his implacable reserve, to jolt his attention from her father's political future to . . . to her? She denied the thought the moment it crossed her mind.

"What do you mean, Stacey?" Justin asked with maddening patience.

"I want to know the correct way to smile at Dad." Oh, to make him lose that dogged patience! "After all, the television cameras will be there and the photographers too. Shall we all smile adoringly or aim for some other kind of smile?"

"Maybe we should practice," Sterne suggested. "At the count of three, everybody flash your most adoring smile."

"How's this?" Lucas gave a Cheshire-cat grin and then whooped with laughter.

"When my daddy takes my picture, I say cheeeeeseburger," announced four-year-old Sunshine.

"And you have a beautiful smile, sweetheart," Spence said, scooping the child up in his arms and kissing her rosy cheek.

Stacey watched her brother and his child closely. Today fathers and children were very much on her mind. Spence was warm and openly affectionate with his daughters. He'd shared childcare chores with Patty since the babies were born. Stacey tried to remember her own father spontaneously picking her up or kissing her. If he ever had, she had no recollection of it. Bradford Lipton projected a charismatic warmth that won him countless admirers, but in private, alone with his family, he was cold and remote. Stacey had adjusted to the strange contrast at an early age and learned to use it. When she wanted or needed something from her father, she was careful to approach him when he was surrounded by reporters or fellow politicians. With an audience, Bradford Lipton could easily project the image of a doting father. Alone, there was no communication or rapport.

"If we can dispense with the levity?" Justin said with a frown. "Time is running short and I haven't finished briefing you."

Stacey absently placed her hand on her abdomen and thought of the child within. Justin Marks's child. What kind of a father would *he* make? If her own father was cold in private, at least he projected an aura of warmth in public. Justin Marks was coolly controlled and impenetrably aloof in public. He was probably as deliberately distancing as the senator in private. She shivered.

Stacey, darling, please open the door. I want to hold you. I know you're upset. Open the door and let me hold you. Once again, she heard Justin's voice running through her brain, and for a moment, she was catapulted back to last August. She had barricaded herself in the bathroom in hysterics while Justin tried to coax her out. But she hadn't listened to him—or had she? Her brain seemed to have taped whatever he'd said and insisted on playing it back to her, unbidden.

She looked at the controlled countenance of the man standing before them and was filled with a terrible confusion. Cool and unapproachable in public, but warm and passionate in private? She couldn't come to grips with it, not after a lifetime with Bradford Lipton.

"Nurse, Mommy!" demanded three-year-old Melody. Patty immediately sat down, unbuttoned her blouse, took the child on her lap, and offered her the breast. Another of Patty and Spence's beliefs was breast-feeding on demand. Age didn't seem to matter to them.

But it did to Justin. "Oh, for heaven's sake," he said, his face reddening.

"You don't approve of a mother nursing her child, Marks?" Spence asked belligerently. "Breast-feeding is perfectly natural and a beautiful, awe-inspiring sight to behold."

"I have no objection to a mother nursing her infant in a public place, provided it's appropriately discreet," Justin replied, exasperated. "But that child can talk! She has a full set of teeth! And I do not think that nursing anyone is appropriate in the middle of the Senate Caucus Room in the presence of the worldwide press!"

"Oh, Melody will be finished by then," Patty said serenely.

Justin took no comfort in that fact. "But what if one of the other ones starts?" He glanced rather desperately at his watch. "It's time to go to the Caucus Room. I have to call Senator and Mrs. Lipton."

Sterne and Lucas were howling with laughter. Normally, Stacey would have been too. Seeing Justin Marks lose his legendary cool was always a treat for Senator Lipton's offspring. And they were the only ones capable of making it happen.

But the topic of infants and nursing was dangerously close to Stacey's terrifying dilemma. Her eyes were riveted to Justin as he entered the senator's luxurious inner office. Justin Marks was hailed as a genius in predicting trends and anticipating public response. He was alert to every nuance in the endless polls he commissioned. Could he predict and anticipate the public reaction to the news of Senator Lipton's daughter's illegitimate pregnancy? And what would be his own personal reaction to the news of his impending fatherhood?

Stacey's heart began to thud wildly against her ribs. Could the child she carried actually damage her father's chances for the presidency? There had never been a breath of scandal attached to Bradford Lipton; he had the image of a warm, highly moral, Midwestern family man. And Justin Marks, with his aggressive marketing skills, had projected and enhanced the senator's image. What were these two men going to say when she told them that she was pregnant? By Justin Marks! She felt the bile rise in her throat. She couldn't tell them, not either of them. She wouldn't!

The door of the inner office opened. Justin appeared and said with a flourish, "Ladies and gentlemen, Senator and Mrs. Bradford Sterne Lipton."

The entire staff began to applaud enthusiastically, along with Justin. "I think Dad is practicing for the White House Inaugural already," Sterne whispered to Stacey. "Look at him flash those choppers."

Stacey stared at her father, so elegantly handsome in his custom-tailored blue suit. He already projected the image of a distinguished head of state. At fifty-four, he possessed an appeal that spanned the generations. Stacey had seen teenage girls jumping and squealing at the sight of him, and middle-aged women gazing rapturously at him as they reached for his hand. Yet the senator was a "man's man" as well, knowledgeable about sports and capable of telling a slightly risqué story while remaining the bastion of old-fashioned values. Did he *really* have a chance to be President? she wondered. Sometimes her father seemed as unreal to Stacey as a highly celebrated media star she'd never met.

The office was crowded now. Other senatorial staff members and several reporters had joined the group. "I'm very appreciative of this," Senator Lipton said, the warmth of his smile encompassing everyone in the office. "And I intend to justify the faith you've shown in me. Having my family's sustained love and support is the backbone of my commitment to the American people."

"Nice, personal little chat with his family, huh?" Spence whispered bitterly. "If the crowd weren't here, he'd walk right past us without a word."

Senator Lipton caught Stacey's eye and winked at her. She blew him a kiss and the whole interaction was duly recorded on videotape. Stacey knew why her father had singled her out for attention. He'd once told Justin that she was the only one of his children who could "skillfully play to the media." He thought she possessed "an excellent sense of theater." They played the roles of father and daughter quite well with an audience present. Stacey went along with it for her own amusement. It was one small way to control a life governed by uncontrollable circumstances.

She stepped back, only to collide with Justin Marks. He'd joined the crowd and was standing directly in back of her. Before she could dart away, he placed both hands on her shoulders, ostensibly to steady her.

For a moment, Stacey stood stock-still as his big hands cupped her shoulders. A sudden wave of heat surged through her and she resisted the insane, impulsive urge to lean back against him. She was achingly aware of the warmth of his hard frame behind her, of the strength in the hands that held her. Her head did not quite reach his chin, and it seemed to fit perfectly within the hollow of his shoulder. She felt warm and safe and secure and—Was she losing her mind? She must be on the verge of it, to be standing there contemplating snuggling up to Justin Marks! She'd been right to keep her distance from him these past two and a half months. She was obviously vulnerable to him in a frightening, physical way.

She moved away from him abruptly, her whole body flushed as if with fever. Thankfully, everyone else in the room was watching the senator, who'd just made a jocular remark.

"Is this one of the jokes we're supposed to laugh at, Stacey?" Lucas asked her in a whisper. "Justin Marks said there would be two."

"There will be two in the Senate Caucus Room," Stacey told him. Justin had once commented that he feared Lucas Lipton had played one too many games of football without his helmet. Stacey had refuted it hotly, but privately she tended to agree. Her youngest brother was clearly not a mental giant. "Just watch me and laugh when I do, Lucas," she murmured.

"It's time to leave," Justin announced, and he motioned the group to step aside and make way for the senator and his wife. They proceeded en masse to the Senate Caucus Room.

"You're looking particularly pretty today, Stacey," Caroline Courtney Lipton said, pausing to wait for her daughter.

"Thanks, Mom." Stacey smiled at her. Her mother was too tactful ever to admit the truth. "But I'm afraid that mustard really isn't my color."

"But your face just seems to have a special glow, darling. A certain radiance," replied her mother.

"Stacey, your face *does* look different, somehow," Patty put in. She was walking beside

Spence, carrying little Aurora, and she studied Stacey thoughtfully.

"I've switched to a new makeup," Stacey said quickly. She remembered that Spence always claimed he could detect a woman in early pregnancy by a "certain something" in her face. Hopefully, he wouldn't notice anything different about his sister. "Mother, you look absolutely wonderful today!" she exclaimed in a quick change of subject.

Caroline Lipton smiled her appreciation. Stacey had often thought her mother had a Mona Lisa-type smile. Feminine and warm, yet reserved, with an air of mystery. Stacey adored her—and was in awe of her too. Her mother had raised the four Liptons single-handedly while her husband devoted himself to his political career. She'd never uttered a word of complaint about the incredible demands upon her time or Bradford Lipton's constant unavailability through the years. At forty-seven, she was still lithe and blonde, and as pretty as she had been at the age of twenty-one, when she'd married Congressman Lipton and taken on full responsibility for his two small sons, Sterne and Spencer.

But though her mother had opted for such a marriage, Stacey had decided years ago that it was not for her. She had solmenly promised herself that she would never, *ever* be trapped in a one-sided marriage in the selfish, hypocritical world of politics.

As they approached the Caucus Room, Senator Lipton stopped and looked behind him. "Caroline?" he said. His face was tense, his blue eyes cold and hard.

Caroline Lipton smiled and took her husband's arm. They entered the room for the historic announcement, and the rest of the Liptons shuffled in, as directed by Justin Marks.

* * *

Stacey's tawny-brown eyes swept the crowd assembled in the Senate Caucus Room, the same room in which John F. Kennedy had announced his candidacy years ago. There were a number of chairs set up and some people were seated, but most of the reporters were on their feet, equipped with notebooks and cameras. All three networks and the local TV and radio stations had sent sound people and video cameras.

Brynn was chatting with a man whom Stacey recognized as a local anchorman. She waved to Stacey and Stacey waved back. A hush fell over the room as Senator Lipton, smiling congenially, began to speak.

It was warm in the room, suffocatingly warm. Ten minutes into her father's speech, Stacey wondered if the ventilation system had broken down. She felt miserably hot, and there didn't seem to be any air circulating. She drew a deep breath and then another, but it didn't help. There was no air! She glanced at her father, who appeared vigorous and dynamic as he spoke. Her mother looked as poised and cool as ever too. Didn't anyone realize that they were all about to suffocate? Stacey wondered.

Her face was hot and flushed, and a sudden wave of nausea swept over her. She could hear her father's voice, but his words weren't making any sense to her. There was a peculiar buzzing in her head. Her gaze darted frantically around the room and collided with the piercing black eyes of Justin Marks. He stood about fifteen feet away from her, and he *should* have been watching Bradford Lipton, but he wasn't. His dark, dark eyes were fixed on her.

She couldn't seem to look away from him. Faintness was rapidly overtaking her. She felt dizzy and weak and a roaring heat filled her ears. She was going to be sick, she realized with dawning horror. Or else she was going to faint. Either prospect was appalling. Her father would certainly revise his opinion on her "excellent sense of theater" if she were to interrupt his moment in the media spotlight by becoming physically ill.

She had to sit down, she thought. She was desperate to close her eyes against the sickening swirls of greens and yellows that were beginning to obstruct her vision. She heard applause and realized that her father's announcement had been made. He was instructing the members of the press corps to ask him whatever questions they wished. Desperately, she started toward Brynn. Brynn would give her her seat. And she simply *had* to sit down. . . .

She felt a strong arm go round her shoulders and her knees buckled. Incredibly, it didn't seem to matter. She didn't fall and her feet kept right on moving. Justin Marks was holding her up, propelling her toward an isolated corner in the back of the room. He sat her down in a chair and his big hand closed around the nape of her neck and forced her head down, down to her knees. Stacey closed her eyes against a nauseating rush of dizziness. She felt alternately hot and cold, and a fine sheen of perspiration bathed her entire body.

"Try to breathe deeply, Stacey." Justin's voice barely penetrated the thick fog that enveloped her, but she tried to obey and gulped in deep breaths of air.

She had no idea how long she sat there, with her eyes closed and her head between her knees. But slowly, gradually, the nausea and the faintness began to subside. The roaring in her head ceased and she was able to swallow. She tuned back into her surroundings. A reporter was asking a question. Her father replied with a quip, and there was laughter throughout the room. She opened her eyes and tried to raise her head.

"Relax, Stacey. Breathe deeply and raise your head very slowly."

She carefully lifted her head and found herself at eye level with Justin. He was down on his haunches beside her chair, his fingers still clamped around the back of her neck. "I'm sorry," she whispered. Her lips were dry and her mouth felt as if it were stuffed with cotton gauze. "Did— did anyone notice?" Her father and his national campaign manager would be justifiably furious if anything were to divert attention from the candidate at such a moment.

"You were most discreet, Stacey. If your departure was noticed at all, it didn't cause a ripple. What happened? Have you been ill?"

"No. I was feeling fine, and all of a sudden I felt faint." A not at all uncommon occurrence in pregnancy, she thought bleakly. What if it were to happen over and over again?

"The heat, the crowd, the excitement," Justin murmured. Stacey guessed he was formulating an answer, should anyone comment about her abrupt departure. She didn't bother to point out that she'd attended political rallies in the middle of hot Nebraska summers since the age of two and had never once succumbed to the heat, the crowds, and the excitement.

His fingers were methodically massaging her neck and he didn't move from his position close beside her. "You looked so sick, Stacey. Your face was chalky white."

She brushed her fingers through her bangs, which were soaked with perspiration. "An improvement over sallow, perhaps?" she said, attempting a small joke.

Justin didn't laugh. "Do you feel well enough to sit up? Do you think you could take some water?"

"Yes. Yes, I think so." She slowly straightened in her chair. The room had stopped spinning. Although she still felt shaky and weak, she knew the acute phase had passed. Justin continued to crouch beside her chair, but he was no longer touching her. He was being amazingly understanding about all this, Stacey thought with real surprise.

"Stacey, are you all right?" Brynn joined them, her face reflecting her concern. She had managed to work her way unobtrusively through the room to Stacey's side. She touched Stacey's damp hair. "Did you faint?"

"Almost." Stacey managed a small smile.

"Brynn, let's get Stacey to my office," Justin said.

"No, I'll be all right," Stacey said quickly. "You stay here and listen to the rest of the press conference, Justin. Brynn and I will go on back to our apartment."

"I can watch the whole thing on videotape later. You're coming to my office, Stacey." Justin had reverted to his usual commanding self. He slipped his hands under her arms and lifted Stacey to her feet as easily as he might lift a rag doll. His effortless strength stunned her, reminding her of the way he had carried her from the banquet hall that warm August night.

They walked down the long corridor to the Senate Office Building, Stacey between Justin and Brynn, each of them supporting her. "Poor Stacey has been feeling sick all day," Brynn said nervously. "Some kind of virus, huh, Stace?"

Stacey sucked in her cheeks. She knew that

Brynn was attempting to explain the fainting episode. Unfortunately, she had directly contradicted Stacey's version of her health.

Justin picked up on it at once, of course. Nothing ever escaped him. "Stacey said she'd been fine and suddenly felt faint," he said.

"Oh!" Brynn gave a nervous little cough. "Well, you know Stacey. She'll never admit to being sick, will you, Stace? What a trooper!"

Stacey lost her footing and accidentally stumbled. "Stace!" Brynn cried, tightening her grip. "Don't fall!"

"I'm all right, Brynn, honestly," Stacey said, attempting to reassure her. If they weren't careful, Justin was going to pick up on Brynn's uncharacteristic nervousness. The man had the cunning of a weasel.

"I'm going to carry you," Justin announced, and before Stacey could utter a word of protest, he'd scooped her up in his arms.

"Put me down!" She demanded through clenched teeth. "I'm perfectly fine!"

"I don't think you are," he replied in that authoritative tone of his. "I'm carrying you to my office. Brynn, go back to the Caucus Room and tell Mrs. Lipton where I've taken Stacey. She can join us there after the senator is finished."

Brynn scurried back down the hall. "People are staring, Justin," Stacey said in a low voice, turning her face into the lapels of his inevitable charcoal-gray suit jacket. "Put me down!" He ignored her protest. "Were you really sick today, Stacey? Why didn't you say something?"

"I wanted to be here when my father announced his candidacy." Justin seemed to have accepted Brynn's tale, and Stacey decided to go along with it. "That's me, the trooper."

He frowned. "Have you seen a doctor?"

Stacey panicked. "See a doctor for a twenty-four-hour bug? No way! Brynn had it yesterday and she feels marvelous today."

They arrived back at Senator Lipton's office suite and Justin carried her past the surprised receptionist and into his own office. He set her down on a reclining chair upholstered in—what else?—charcoal gray.

"Just sit there and relax, Stacey. I'll bring you some water." He walked over to the water cooler in the corner of his office and plucked a paper cup from a dispenser on the wall.

"You have your own water cooler?" Stacey asked curiously.

"I rent the cooler and the company supplies me with fresh drinking water every week. They replace this gallon jug." He smiled and her heart gave a queer little lurch. "I go through two or three gallons a week. I guess you could call it my secret vice."

"Drinking water is your secret vice?" She leaned back in the chair. It was surprisingly comfortable. She knew Justin didn't drink, smoke, gamble, or womanize. His lack of vices appalled Sterne, who indulged in them all. "So Justin Marks has a weakness, after all." She couldn't resist teasing him. "He drinks water."

"You're smiling." Justin stood above her, cup of water in hand. "You *are* feeling better."

She took the water and gulped it gratefully. "May I have more, please?" she asked, handing him the empty cup.

"Aha! You're getting hooked on it too." He brought her a refill. "I used to drink coffee by the potful. Two years ago, a doctor advised me to give it up, and I had this cooler installed. Now I drink water just as compulsively."

She was surprised by the personal revelation.

Justin Marks made a practice of never divulging anything about himself. "And you don't miss the coffee?"

"Oh, I miss coffee. Terribly. But I didn't want the ulcers the doctors promised I'd have if I didn't cut down on it."

"So instead of merely cutting down on coffee, you gave it up completely. The old all-or-nothing approach to life, hmm? That sounds just like you, Justin."

"I also know how and when to compromise, Stacey," he said quietly. Stacey flushed. She had the uneasy feeling he was not talking about coffee consumption any longer. Her gaze connected with the framed 8″ × 10″ color photograph on his desk. It was the Lipton family, the same picture she kept in her bedroom.

Justin followed her gaze. "We've scheduled a photographer to take an updated family portrait over the Thanksgiving weekend. It will be reprinted in a pamphlet outlining the senator's position. . . ."

He continued to talk, but Stacey paid scant attention. Listening to campaign strategy tended to make her eyes glaze. She stared at the framed photographs that nearly filled the four walls of the office. Her father was in every picture, with the president or congressional leaders or foreign heads of state, with religious leaders and sports heroes and Hollywood stars. All the pictures were autographed by the people in them, except the eight on the wall directly behind Justin's desk.

Stacey's eyes widened as she stared at those eight pictures. They were all of *her*, at varying ages, with her father. She was shown as a dimpled baby, as a toothless Brownie, as a high-school cheerleader, as a preppily dressed college coed. And there was a picture of her at age seventeen, wearing the beribboned, white-ruffled dress that Justin had suggested she wear that August night. The last three pictures were of the adult Stacey. One of her in jeans, laughing into the wind, another of her wearing a sophisticated black silk dress and diamond earrings, looking regal and poised. And the last . . .

Stacey gulped. It had been taken at the Man-of-the-Year award banquet. There she was in her sexy, red cocktail dress and strappy sandals, grinning impishly at her father, who had just told a Stacey-related joke. An excellent sense of theater; both father and daughter possessed it. Justin Marks wasn't in the picture, naturally. He'd been in the background, where he always carefully kept himself.

Stacey's pulse quickened. She was shaken by her unexpected presence in Justin's gallery and equally unnerved by the reminder of that passionate night they'd spent together. Turning quickly, she found him watching her with intent black eyes.

His gaze flicked from the picture taken that night to her apprehensive brown eyes. "It's time to discuss what happened that night, Stacey," he said silkily.

Three

A tremor of fear rippled through Stacey. "No!" she said. "Oh, yes, Stacey." Justin's eyes glittered. "I knew I had to give you time—and space—to accept what happened between us. I knew that after ten years of seeing me as an antagonist, you needed to adjust to the idea of me as your lover. It was most opportune that the past three months have been so demanding in terms of the final organization and preparations for the campaign. I could give you the time and space that you needed. But now—"

"You'll be busier than ever," Stacey interjected quickly. "The Iowa caucuses and the New Hampshire primary are in February. You have to win big there or it'll be all over."

Justin's lips curved into a confident smile. "We *are* going to win big in both. The 'surprise victory' has been two years in the making. Our advance work has been so thorough that the candidate need merely show up, smile, and speak to the crowds."

"Whitney Chambers isn't going to agree with that," she retorted. Whitney Chambers was the popular junior senator from New York who also planned to seek the nomination, although he hadn't formally announced his candidacy yet.

Bradford Lipton had beaten him by one day. There were a dozen others planning to run, too, although the incumbent president hadn't officially endorsed any of them.

"Whit Chambers may be the eastern media favorite, but he's going to lose badly in Iowa and New Hampshire," Justin said with the certainty he might use when stating that Christmas falls on December 25th. "And we're digressing from the issue at hand, Stacey."

"I intend to keep digressing. There is nothing to say about w-what happened that night." She thought of the child growing within her and froze at the bold-faced lie. She couldn't keep her condition secret much longer. And then what? "I want to leave now." Panic propelled her blindly to the door.

Justin blocked the door by standing in front of it. "Not quite yet, Stacey."

She stared at him, trying to marshal her scattered wits. She was being too emotional, she had to regain her cool. If she were to rush at him in an attempt to push him aside, he would grab her to stop her. And Stacey realized in a flash of insight that that was exactly what Justin Marks expected her to do. *Wanted* her to do!

His black eyes challenged her. He wanted an excuse to touch her, she realized nervously. There was more than challenge glowing in his glittering eyes. There was passion. Stacey drew a deep breath and stepped backward. "No! I'm not going to let you touch me, Justin."

He folded his arms across his chest, his face an impassive mask. "I have no intention of touching you until you want me to, Stacey."

"That will be never!"

"Will it?"

"Yes! I don't like you, Justin Marks. I've never liked you and I never will like you."

"Then how do you explain your response to me that night last August?" he asked with his usual maddening logic.

"I was drunk! *You* were, drunk. You don't like me either, remember?"

His eyes flicked to the pictures on the wall behind his desk. "Is that what you think?"

"That's what I know!" she retorted hotly. "You've never approved of me or my brothers. You view us all as albatrosses around Dad's political neck."

Surprisingly, Justin grinned. "I'll admit I've sometimes wished you all had more political savvy. All four of you seem to work at staying remarkably uninformed."

"And we've pulled some classic political gaffes. Remember when Sterne made a pass at the spokeswoman from the National Organization for Women?" Stacey's lips curved into a reluctant smile at the memory. "And the time a student group protested Dad's stand on nuclear weapons to Lucas, and he listened to them in amazement and said—"

" 'Gee, how come Dad wants to do that?' " Justin chimed in and they chorused Lucas's infamous reply. And both ended up laughing. Stacey was surprised by his laughter. Neither Justin nor her father had laughed at the time.

"Then there was the time," Justin said," you went out with the son of your father's wealthiest campaign contributor and confided to a reporter that the kid was a 'real nerd.' "

"I was only sixteen at the time. And the kid *was* a real nerd!"

Justin shook his head, laughing. "So was the kid's father, but it's hardly the kind of thing you tell the press."

Abruptly, Stacey's smile faded. "That's what I particularly despise about politics, Justin. The phoniness, the hypocrisy, the manipulators and the users. It's an artificial world."

"None of that is exclusively consigned to politics, Stacey. I worked in advertising and in marketing in New York City before I joined your father's staff, and the dynamics were the same there. Perhaps even more cutthroat."

Stacey's golden-brown eyes held a faraway look. "I remember so well when you first joined Dad's staff. Dad kept raving about what a genius you were and how lucky he was to have you on his team. He said that we all had to do whatever you told us to do, because you were in complete command." Her face hardened. "We hated you before we ever laid eyes on you. And nothing has changed!"

"Your hostility toward me is all mixed up with your hostility and resentment toward your father, Stacey. I realize that it must have been particularly difficult for your older brothers to watch a man not much older than they become their father's confidante."

"Particularly when Dad scarcely spoke to them," she added grimly.

"And you're very loyal to your brothers, aren't you, Stacey?" Justin said quietly. "I'm sure all four of you found it hard to listen to your father rave on about how lucky he was to have me when he'd never expressed a similar sentiment about his own children. And in my position, I'd been handed the role of giving directions that more suitably might have come from your father himself."

"Except he was too busy to bother with any of us. He never has."

Justin's eyes held hers. "I'm fully aware that ours has been a most difficult relationship thus far, Stacey."

"And will continue to be," she promised coolly.

His analysis of her family secretly astonished her. She'd never credited Justin with a shred of emotional insight. She'd never credited him with a shred of emotion!

"No, Stacey." He gave her a crooked smile. "Our relationship is about to change dramatically. For one thing, we'll be seeing each other constantly. We're going to be working very closely with one another from now on. I've given you three months since that night in August. Plenty of time, plenty of space. It's time to rein you in, butterfly."

"You're talking in metaphors. And you're not making a bit of sense!" She meant to snap at him, her tone forcefully caustic. Stacey was dismayed to hear herself sounding nervous and confused.

"Then let me explain, Stacey." His smile seemed slightly feral, and it chilled her. "As of today you've resigned from your job on Congressman Erlich's staff and joined your father's staff as a full-time campaign worker."

"You're crazy! I didn't resign from my job—and I'm not going to. I told my father years ago that I'd help out when I could, but I'd *never* officially join any of his campaigns full-time."

"Perhaps you've changed your mind since then?" Justin suggested, handing her a typewritten paper from the top of his in-basket.

It was a letter of resignation to Congressman Nicholas Erlich—from her! Stacey gaped at it, then crumpled it into a ball and threw it on the floor. "I'm not resigning! And if a copy of this bogus resignation has already been sent to Nick's office, I'll just tell him it was one of your overzealous mistakes."

"Stacey, Nick Erlich is your father's protégé in the House. He understands the necessity of your presence in your father's presidential campaign.

Perhaps, after the election, you can work in Nick's office again if you should want to."

"I want to work there now!" she exclaimed, seething. "I won't have my life disrupted this way, Justin. If my father chooses to run for president, that's his decision, but I'm not going to change my whole life because of it."

"Stacey." He took a step toward her. "Your job with Nick Erlich no longer exists. It was created for you at your father's request and abolished the same way."

A horrible wave of anxiety washed over her. Her father didn't concern himself with her life. If he had asked Nick Erlich to create a job on his staff for her, it was because Justin Marks had suggested it! She stared at Justin, her eyes reflecting her sudden comprehension. "Why?" she whispered.

He moved closer, until he was standing beside her. He towered over her, and she was breathlessly aware of his hard, muscular frame just a hand's length away. "Think back to your college graduation four years ago, Stacey. You had a liberal arts degree and no useful job skills. You couldn't even type! You and Brynn Cassidy were talking of going to Europe, of working your way around the world." He smiled faintly. "I couldn't allow that to happen. I had to know where you were, to know that you were . . . safe."

"And you arranged that phone call from Nick, asking me to come up to Capitol Hill for an interview?"

"Honey, if you were at all savvy politically, you'd have realized that congressmen don't recruit their staff from people who haven't even applied for a job! Life as a senator's daughter has insulated you somewhat from the real world, you see."

Stacey was speechless. Lord, she had been hopelessly naive, hadn't she? And all the while she'd been manipulated, *controlled*, by Justin Marks! The realization enraged her.

"So now you have a new job, Stacey." His hands hovered above her shoulders for a moment, then settled on them. "You're going to be my own personal aide. You'll receive the same salary you were paid by Erlich and I'll fit a small desk for you right here in my office. From now on, all of your time will be spent with me."

She felt as if she were caught in a dangerous steel trap. "Forget it!" She whirled away from him, her heart pounding. "I won't do it! If Nick won't give me my job back, I really will work my way around the world!" At this time, the idea held great appeal. She could be gone for months, years! She could have this baby quietly, without anyone being the wiser. . . .

"Report to my office tomorrow morning at nine, Stacey," Justin said, completely ignoring her panicky outburst. "I'll be here before eight, of course, but I won't expect you to keep my hours."

"No, Justin!" She paced the office, her movements frenetic. Her father grinned down at her from all those framed photographs on the wall. She felt completely trapped, caged. There wasn't even a window to look out for distraction. "I'll tell my father that I don't want to work with you, that I want to keep my job on Nick Erlich's staff."

Justin remained still, as calm as she was hyperactive. "And I'll tell him that I need you on staff with me. Which one of us do you think he'll back, Stacey?"

Stacey knew all too well. "You and my father can—can take a running leap, Justin Marks," she spluttered in frustration. "No one tells me what to do! If my job with Nick is gone, so be it. I'll find something else to do, something far away." Perhaps it was for the best, she thought. She could disappear out west or in Canada under an assumed name.

"Of course, you do have your trust fund, set up for you by your grandfather Courtney. A tidy little sum that would easily tide you over until you found something you really wanted to do," Justin pointed out in a frighteningly reasonable tone. "You're lucky in that regard, Stacey. It's too bad your friend Brynn doesn't have a similar cushion to fall back on."

Her heart seemed to stop beating, then begin again at a wild pace. "What do you mean, Justin?" She knew him well enough to know that he made no idle remarks.

"I know how close you and Brynn are, Stacey, and I know that Brynn needs her job. So when I got the word that there were to be extensive cuts in the staffs of various House committees—including the House Human Resources Committee, which Brynn works for—I made it a point to look into it." He reached into his desk to retrieve several sheets of paper and handed them to Stacey. "Brynn's position was one of the ones to be axed, Stacey."

"Oh, no!" Stacey was horrified. "Brynn will be crushed! She loves her job, she—"

"She doesn't have to worry about it," Justin cut in calmly." In fact, she doesn't even have to know how close she came to the unemployment line. I intervened with the committee, and used my own influence—as well as your father's—to secure Brynn's job. Another position was eliminated, not hers. Brynn's job is safe, Stacey."

Stacey cast a covert glance at him. His face was a total enigma. Only the hard black eyes called to mind *The Washington Post*'s description of Senator Lipton's longtime administrative assistant: "Ruthless and intense, Marks has the enviable reputation on Capitol Hill of doing whatever is needed to achieve the necessary results."

"You owe me, Stacey. I went out on a limb for your friend and you know how I hate to ask for favors and incur debts. But I did it for you—and Brynn. If I hadn't, she'd already be scanning the want ads in the *Post*."

"I owe you," Stacey repeated in a whisper. "And now you're going to collect?"

"Yes, Stacey, now I'm going to collect." He smiled at her. He had her and they both knew it. He'd saved Brynn's job and now Stacey owed him a favor. No wonder Justin was forever cautioning her about asking for favors in the political world. When one was indebted to another . . .

She decided that she'd never hated anyone as much as she hated Justin Marks at this moment. "Someone is going to lace your water cooler with strychnine, Justin Marks. And I'm going to dance at your funeral."

His smile widened. "I take it you've decided to gracefully accept your new position?"

She drew herself to her full height, which she wished was considerably taller. "You're going to be sorry for this, Justin!" Even to her own ears, she sounded childish and impotent. She had nothing to back up her threats and Justin knew it. "I don't think so, Stacey." He was regarding her with amusement. "Welcome aboard the Lipton campaign trail."

And then it struck her. Nothing to back up her threats? She had the racy tale of a night of wild passion shared by Senator Lipton's daughter and his campaign manager, which had resulted in an out-of-wedlock pregnancy. Wouldn't the "Style" editor of the *Post* be interested in a story like that? Far from being powerless, Stacey possessed the potential to obliterate the Lipton campaign trail.

Her eyes widened in fear. She didn't want that kind of power! She wasn't vindictive and ruthless, and she'd always been sickened by the bloodthirsty politics of revenge.

Justin was watching her, and he saw the range of emotions play across her face. From fury to calculation to outright fear. "Stacey?" He moved toward her, his hard face mirroring his concern. "Are you all right?"

His big hand cupped her cheek. "You're cold," he murmured. "Stacey, you're still feeling sick, aren't you?" His other hand slipped around her shoulders and he guided her to the gray armchair. "I didn't realize . . . Stacey, I didn't mean to upset you. If I'd known you were still feeling sick, I would have—"

"Waited before demanding that my debt be paid?" she asked grimly as she sank into the chair. She wasn't actually physically ill, but she was sick with terror, trapped in circumstances she knew must lead to disaster. "You're all heart, Justin."

"Stacey." He squatted down in front of her, taking both her hands in his. "Someday, someday soon, I hope you'll understand how—"

There was a loud knock at the office door. Justin dropped her hands and stood up. "Come in."

Brynn entered, with Caroline and Lucas in tow. "Hey, Stace. You sick?" Lucas asked around a wad of gum.

"How do you feel, dear?" Caroline looked worried as she hurried to Stacey's side.

"I'm fine, Mother," Stacey reassured her with a smile. She inhaled a whiff of her mother's perfume and felt a perilous urge to lay her head against her mother's breast and cry. But she hadn't done that since she she was a second-grader, and her mother couldn't help her now, anyway.

Her mother would never understand how her

daughter had landed herself in such a fix, Stacey thought, pregnant by a man she'd professed to hate for the past ten years! Caroline Courtney Lipton was perfect in every way. Did her mother want her husband to be president? Stacey wondered. Did she eagerly anticipate becoming First Lady? There were so many questions Stacey had never asked her mother and so much she wanted to understand about her.

They couldn't talk confidentially to each other, though. They never had. Very personal topics were off limits in the Lipton family. It was an unspoken family rule that all of them followed. Tears swam in Stacey's eyes, darkening them to a rich brown. She'd always heard that pregnant women were supposed to be emotional and she seemed to be living proof of it. How could she ever hope to keep her volatile mood swings in check under Justin Marks's scrupulous daily surveillance?

She shivered. The nightmare was already in full swing.

"You have a chill," Caroline said. "Stacey, why don't you come home with me today?" She was referring to the spacious Lipton house in Chevy Chase. "You can go right to bed, and Grace will make you some of her delicious soup. . . ."

"If I didn't have to get back to practice, I'd go," said Lucas, grinning. "You coming to the game on Saturday, Stace?"

"I don't know, Lucas," Stacey said. Occasionally she accompanied her parents to the University of Nebraska football games to watch her brother play. Senator Lipton never missed a game. It was politically expedient for him to be in his home state for the university's games, and for a change one of his children's activities coincided with political opportunity.

"Stacey might be taking care of me by then, if I

catch whatever bug she seems to have," Brynn said, winking at Stacey.

"Stacey told me you had this bug—or whatever it is—yesterday," Justin said, frowning.

Brynn's face reddened. "Oh! Oh, yes, I did. I—er—forgot."

Stacey suppressed a groan. Caroline and Justin exchanged speculative glances. Stacey and Brynn exchanged apprehensive ones.

"You forgot you were sick yesterday?" Even Lucas picked up on that one.

"There is something not quite right here." Justin glanced from Stacey to Brynn, his frown deepening. "Are you going to tell me what it is? Or shall I find out for myself?"

"I don't know what he's talking about. Do you know what he's talking about, Stace?" Brynn was beginning to panic. Stacey recognized the signs. Poor Brynn always talked too much and too fast when she was nervous. "So I forgot I was sick yesterday! So sue me! I mean, with all the excitement about Senator—"

"Mother, please tell Justin to drop his overbearing, arrogant high-handedness," Stacey cut in. Taking a cue from Lucas's playbook, she decided a good defense was sometimes a strong offense. Or something to that effect. "He's upsetting Brynn."

"Why don't you tell me yourself, Stacey?" Justin suggested softly. "While I drive you home?"

"No one is driving me anywhere. I have my own car and I'm driving myself to Sterne's Place. He invited me over for a bacon cheeseburger on the house."

"That's awfully greasy, Stace," Brynn said. "I think something like baked chicken, vegetables, and milk would be much more healthful for you— uh—at this time."

Stacey flashed Brynn a warning look. "I love Sterne's bacon cheeseburgers, Brynnie."

"Stacey, you're not coming home?" Caroline sounded distressed.

"Stacey, you're *not* going to that meat market of Sterne's!" Justin sounded emphatic.

"Sterne's Place isn't a meat market," Stacey protested. "At least not at five-thirty in the afternoon. And, Mom, I'm perfectly all right." She had to get out of here—now! "I'd better be on my way. 'Bye, Mom. 'Bye, Lucas. Come on, Brynn."

"Stacey!" Justin called as she rushed out the door.

"I know, I know. Nine o'clock tomorrow morning," she called over her shoulder without a backward glance.

"Are you crazy? You can't work for Justin Marks, Stacey!" Brynn said as they dashed through the cold November drizzle toward their cars. "You're going to have his baby in six months. Don't you think he'll notice when you show up in the office wearing maternity clothes?"

"I didn't have a choice, Brynn. He made me an offer I couldn't refuse." They had reached Stacey's car, a sporty blue BMW and another bone of contention between her and Justin. He thought it imperative that everyone connected with Senator Lipton drive an American car in support of the senator's "Buy American" slogan. Stacey might have done just that if Justin hadn't told her that she *had* to. Thus, her German-made BMW.

"Stace, are you going to tell him?" Brynn asked slowly.

"No! Brynn, if I were to tell Justin Marks that I'm pregnant, what do you think he'd do?"

"Accuse you of conspiring with the opposition to destroy your father's candidacy?"

"Probably. But if he knew I'm pregnant with his child, he'd insist on marrying me, for the sake of the campaign. And I do *not* want to be married to a man with microchips instead of brain cells and floppy discs rather than emotions. And I loathe politics, Brynn! I have no intention of plunging myself—and an innocent child—into life with a political mastermind whose sole interest in life is making my father president."

"Maybe the baby won't mind," Brynn suggested in a stab at humor. "After all, it is Justin Marks's child. Maybe it will be born tabulating delegate counts."

Stacey shuddered. "I've lived my whole life in a home dominated by politics and I've watched my father's obsession hurt our family, especially Sterne and Spence. The only reason the four of us are at all sane is because my mother selflessly devoted her life to us when we were young. And at least my mother loves my father . . . I think. Whether he loves her or not is anybody's guess, but I already know Justin Marks doesn't love me and never will. A marriage between us would be even worse than my parents' marriage! And I *never* wanted a political marriage like theirs."

The two were silent a moment. Brynn was the first to speak again. "Stacey, maybe Justin Marks cares more for you than you think. The way he jumped to his feet and ran to you today when you almost fainted. . ."

"What choice did he have, Brynn? If I'd fainted flat on the floor, it would've certainly disrupted my father's big moment."

"But he scarcely glanced at your father, Stacey. His eyes were fixed on you. I should know—I spent the entire time watching him watch you. He never took his eyes off you. I think he has the hots for you, Stace."

Stacey laughed at that. "The only thing that makes Justin Marks hot is political tracts and commanding leads in the polls."

"I don't know about that, Stace. You must've done a darn good job of it that night in August."

Stacey blushed. Images of that night tumbled through her brain and she instinctively clutched at her abdomen. She'd done more than physically arouse Justin that night—she'd conceived his child. She was going to have a baby! It still didn't seem possible, but she knew it was true.

"Are you really going to Sterne's, Stacey? I have a date, but I can break it if you want to go home and talk," Brynn offered.

Stacey pulled herself together. She had to. "Sterne really did invite me over, Brynn. And don't break your date. I'm okay, honestly."

"If you're sure . . ." Brynn looked doubtful.

"I'm sure, Brynnie. I'll see you later tonight. And have a good time!" Stacey added, hoping she sounded cheerier than she felt.

"You mean you invited me over here to talk to a reporter?" Stacey asked, glowering at her brother. Sterne's Place, usually crowded and noisy late on weekend nights, was empty this rainy night, with the exception of one customer. It was a man, seated at a small table near a mirrored wall. He was wearing a beige raincoat and puffing laconically on an ivory-carved Turkish pipe.

Stacey recognized the man at once. It was Cord Marshall, the investigative-journalist host of a local TV station's news show, dubbed by its detractors as an audio-visual *National Enquirer.* Cord Marshall was persona non grata to nearly everyone in public life in Washington, but his show held ratings that broke all records in the area. Sometimes items disclosed on his show received national attention, and rumor had it that all three major networks were interested in this local phenomenon.

"And he's not even a reporter!" Stacey hissed crossly. "He's a muckraker!" Just what she needed at this point! "Thanks a lot, Sterne!"

"Aw, Stace, Marshall's all right. And he promised to feature Sterne's Place in a segment on his show if I arranged a meeting with you. Publicity like that could send business through the roof, Stacey."

"If I don't send you there first," muttered Stacey. She should've guessed that Sterne had some ulterior motive besides brotherly confidences when he'd invited her here. Though Sterne was close to no one, Stacey never stopped hoping for a deeper, closer relationship with him. But she should have known better. No one in their fractured family was really close to another. And now she had to deal with Cord Marshall! Ugh! "Well, as long as I'm here, I may as well talk to the slug," she grumbled. "Since he went to all the trouble of crawling out from under his rock." She started across the room.

"Stacey Lipton!" Cord Marshall was on his feet as she approached, extending his hand to her. He was a handsome man in his late thirties, and he smiled in what Stacey assumed was supposed to be a welcoming manner. She rather thought he looked liked the spider greeting the fly. Justin was going to be apoplectic when he'd heard she had met with Cord Marshall, of all people!

The thought suddenly cheered her and she flashed a defiant smile. "Hello, Mr. Marshall."

"Call me Cord, please, Stacey," he said smoothly. "I'm so glad you came tonight. All my sources told me that the Lipton family never did interviews by order of the Emperor Justinian."

It was true. Justin refused to allow Stacey and her brothers to do personal interviews because they were so terrible at it. Inevitably, one of them would say or do something to embarrass or infuriate their father.

"I didn't come for an interview, Cord." She smiled sweetly. "I came for a bacon cheeseburger."

"As did I." Cord Marshall pulled out a chair for her. "Your brother assures me he makes the best bacon cheeseburgers in D.C. Sit down, Stacey. Would you like a drink?"

She almost ordered an amaretto sour, but paused. Alcohol might not be wise, not with a baby inside her—and not with a professional snoop across the table from her! "Just a ginger ale, please."

Marshall arched his dark brows, but said nothing. Sterne insisted on serving him a Scotch on the rocks. On the house.

"Stacey, I'm not here to interview you." Marshall leaned toward her, his vivid blue eyes fixed upon her. "I'd like to invite you to be a guest on my show. This Saturday."

Sterne, who was lurking around the table after serving the drinks, burst into laughter. "You must be kidding, Marshall! he said. "Justin Marks would arrange a power outage or blow up your studio before he'd allow one of the loose-lipped Liptons to appear on your show. Anyway, my sister doesn't deserve one of your hatchet jobs. She's a good kid."

Those were high words of praise from Sterne. Stacey smiled at him appreciatively.

"I'm not going to do a hatchet job on Stacey—or anyone." Marshall seemed to be trying to look hurt. "My idea is to have the daughters of the presidential hopefuls together on a show and have them compare experiences on what it's like being the daughter of a man who wants to be president. Et cetera, et cetera. It's a human-interest story, timeless and perfectly harmless."

Actually, it didn't seem very dangerous to Stacey. Wasn't there safety in numbers? "Do you have anyone lined up yet?" she asked.

Marshall nodded. "Laura Chambers has already agreed and so have the daughters of five of the other top hopefuls."

"I don't believe you," countered Stacey. "I think that I'm the first one you've contacted and if I say yes, you'll use my name and the same line on all the others."

"You're sharp, Stacey," Marshall said admiringly. "And you're absolutely right, of course. Will you do it?"

"You'd better run it by Justin Marks first, Stacey," Sterne cautioned. "You know he won't approve of it and—"

"The man isn't my keeper, Sterne," Stacey said. It was the wrong time for him to have brought up Justin Marks's power over their lives. She thought of her abolished job and her new one, at his side. "I can do whatever I please *without* running it by Justin Marks. And if he doesn't approve, too bad!"

"Bravo, Stacey!" Cord Marshall applauded. "I like to see a woman assert herself. And I promise you that the show will be done with taste and dignity."

"Coming from the man who produced such shows as 'Overweight Teen Bludgeons Parents and then Raids Refrigerator,' I don't feel especially reassured, Mr. Marshall. And I didn't say I'd do it anyway."

"Call me Cord," he insisted. "Hey, Stacey, why don't we skip your brother's greasy spoon cheeseburgers for a decent meal? Let me take you to Harvey's for seafood."

"Greasy spoon?" protested Sterne. "Not so, Marshall."

Why not? Stacey thought recklessly. She liked Harvey's, and it had been a while since she'd been there. And visualizing Justin Marks's horror when he learned she'd had dinner with Cord Marshall made the offer irresistible. "Only if you promise me that everything we say will be off the record . . . Cord," Stacey cooed, smiling sweetly.

Stacey arrived back at her apartment shortly before ten o'clock. Surprisingly, she'd had a pleasant evening with Cord Marshall. The food had been delicious and he hadn't probed or antagonized or tried to trip her up with trick questions. Justin would never believe it, but she and Cord had talked football, pro and college, all through dinner. Cord was an avid fan and Stacey, having grown up with the equally fanatic Lucas, was quite knowledgeable on the subject. Had Cord Marshall taped their conversation, nothing detrimental to Senator Lipton would have surfaced.

Stacey showered and slipped into her long, ivory-colored velour robe. She was exhausted, but too mentally keyed up to sleep. She wished Brynn were there; she wanted to talk. She *needed* to talk. She ran her fingers through her thick brown hair, tousling it slightly, as she restlessly paced the small living room. Countless images of the events of the day flashed wildly before her mind's eye.

The pregnancy test, her father's announcement, Justin carrying her into his office, his black, black eyes watching her, always watching her. What if their child had those watchful black eyes?

The sound of the doorbell jarred her from her

rather incoherent reverie. She padded to the door and carefully peered through the peephole, an automatic precaution with her. Justin Marks was standing in the hall outside the door. She froze, seemingly unable to move or breathe.

"I know you're in there, Stacey," he said calmly to the closed door. "You're cowering behind the door, hoping that I'll leave if you don't answer the bell." He pressed the bell again. "I'm not going to leave, Stacey."

She flung open the door. "I wasn't cowering! I never cower!"

"No, you don't, do you?" He stared down at her with an amused smile. "Feisty little Stacey."

In her bare feet, with him towering nearly a full foot over her, Stacey felt her lack of height and resented it mightily. "And I'm not little, either!"

Justin stepped inside. He was wearing—what else?—a charcoal-gray suit, white shirt, and dark blue tie. His black wing-tip shoes were immaculately polished and shined, as usual. Stacey folded her arms across her chest in the classic defensive position and asked sternly, "What are you doing here, Justin?"

"I came to make sure you were all right." He stared down at her with those piercing eyes. "When I called Sterne to make sure you'd arrived at his bar safely, he seemed to have developed amnesia. He couldn't remember if he'd seen you there tonight."

Sterne would *not* want to be the one to tell Justin Marks that she had gone to dinner with Cord Marshall, Stacey thought. Sterne the chicken-hearted, Spence used to call the eldest Lipton son. It seemed the name still applied. "Well, I was there," she said.

"Yes, Sterne finally remembered, with some prompting. He said you'd left to go to dinner with a man you met there." Justin's face was a cool, impassive mask, his tone equally controlled. But a fire was burning in his coal-black eyes, and Stacey lost some of her determined bravado. She forced herself to face him steadily.

"I did. I had dinner with Cord Marshall at Harvey's. We had a marvelous meal," she added.

Justin's face was no longer impassive. "Marshall? That muckraker? That garbage-scrounger? You had dinner with *him?*"

It was thrilling when Justin dropped his usual remote reserve. Stacey was inspired to new heights. "Cord and I had a lovely time. He invited me to be on his show on Saturday, and I accepted."

Standing directly in front of her, Justin bore a marked resemblance to a thundering, dark giant. "You're joking, aren't you, Stacey?" His expression told her that he didn't find the joke humorous in the least.

"No." She drew back a little. He was too close, far too close. "And you needn't worry, Justin. The show is going to be in good taste, with myself and the daughters of six other presidential hopefuls discussing their lives with—"

"It's a trap!" Justin interrupted furiously. "Dammit, Stacey, a man who goes through people's garbage is incapable of good taste. And he does, you know. He actually searches people's garbage cans for whatever he can find out about them." He flexed his fingers, and Stacey guessed that he wanted to throttle her. He took a step nearer, and before she could back away he caught her arms and anchored her firmly in place. "I'll call Marshall and cancel your appearance. And you are not to see or speak to the man again, Stacey."

"I'll choose my own friends, Justin. I always have. And I *am* going to do that show. It'll be perfectly harmless and I've given my word." Cord

Marshall had admired her assertive spirit, she reminded herself. She would not knuckle under to a decree by the Emperor Justinian. She tried to pull out of his grasp, but he didn't release her.

"You did it for revenge, didn't you?" he said in a low voice. His breathing was rapid and erratic. "Because of the job change? And once Marshall has you in front of the camera—"

"I'll do just fine," she interrupted him fiercely. She tried again to pull away from him, for she was acutely aware of the heat emanating from his strong, masculine frame. "Remember my excellent sense of theater?"

"Stacey, Marshall is going to want your *own* opinion on every controversial issue of the day. And he is a past master at getting people to say what they don't necessarily mean. He could make Mother Teresa sound shady. He is a conniving manipulator, Stacey." Justin's grip on her tightened.

"I won't tell him anything, Justin. I'll just say that I pay no attention to politics, that my motto is 'Girls Just Want to Have Fun.'" She put her hands on his chest and gave a hard push, catching him completely off guard. Justin lost his balance and fell sideways onto the sofa.

She started to laugh; she couldn't help herself. The sight of the always dignified Justin Marks sprawled on the sofa would make a picture worthy of use on *The Cord Marshall Show.* She was laughing so hard that she didn't see his hand snake out to seize her wrist. He gave a sharp tug and she tumbled down beside him on the sofa, her arms and legs askew. Her laughter ended abruptly.

"Don't be so rough, Justin!" Even to her own ears, she sounded like a bossy little girl ordering her brother around. She had once been exactly that. "I shouldn't be tossed around like—like a beach ball!" she added with an attempt at frozen dignity. Not in her condition—for which *he* was responsible!

A wild fury suddenly flared through her. She tried to get up, but Justin moved as swiftly and smoothly as a dark panther. One of his long legs trapped both of hers and his hands closed over her shoulders, pushing her back against the cushions.

"You can dish it out, but you sure can't take it, Stacey Lynn Lipton," he taunted softly.

"Let me up!" She pushed at him with both hands. The hem of her robe had slipped above her knees and she kicked her legs, but the solid anchor of his thighs rendered her efforts useless. Beneath her hands, she could feel the flexing of his muscles as he held her down. The warm weight of his body pressed into hers and within a matter of moments, Stacey was swept from fury to quivering sexual awareness.

"I can't, Stacey," he said, his voice no longer teasing. Her gaze flew to his face. He was staring at her, a look of raw hunger blazing in his ebony eyes. His gaze electrified her, and she felt a tight, sweet ache in her midsection that radiated a glowing heat to the very core of her.

"I can't let you go," he said hoarsely. "I have to hold you, Stacey. I have to touch you. I can't wait any longer."

She held her breath as his fingertips gently stroked her cheek, then traced the line of her jaw down to her throat. He touched her as if she were delicate porcelain, fragile and precious. His lips replaced his fingers in the tender exploration, and he pressed butterfly-soft kisses on her eyelids, her cheeks, her throat.

"Justin." She whispered his name as if in a trance. Her hands trembling, she skimmed her fingers over his high cheekbones. She felt the slightly rough skin of his jaw and heard him draw a ragged breath. With him settled intimately against her, she was fully aware of his tense masculine arousal. A liquid heaviness throbbed deeply within her and she expelled her breath on a sigh.

She watched his mouth descend toward hers with an unbearably exciting sense of anticipation. He really did have the most beautifully shaped and sensual mouth, she thought dizzily. And she was suddenly desperate for the feel of that mouth on hers. Her lips, her arms, her whole body was clamoring for him.

His mouth came down on hers with a breath-taking impact. The taste of him was heady. Her lips parted for his tongue, which surged, bold and insistent, into her mouth. He tasted her deeply, possessively, and she threaded her fingers through his hair and hungrily kissed him back. She was starving for him, wild for him, needing him with a force she'd never known. Never had she responded so volatilely to a man's kiss, not even to Justin himself on that climactic August night. Now she seemed to crave him with her whole being, her needs heightened and more intensified. She wanted to be part of him in a most elemental way.

Again and again his mouth took hers, demanding and receiving her intimate, passionate response. His hand closed masterfully over her breast, his fingers seeking the nipple, peaked hard with arousal. She winced with unexpected discomfort. Her breasts were particularly tender these days and her nipples felt tingling and sore.

"Don't," she whispered as he rubbed the swollen softness with his palm.

"Why not, darling? You love me to touch your breasts." His evocative words, the huskiness of his voice, left her reeling on the brink of intoxicating excitement. But his hands, though ardent and arousing, hurt her breasts, sore today from the caprices of her pregnancy.

"It . . . They—they're sore," she said haltingly, her face scarlet.

For just a split second, Justin looked puzzled, and then a smile of comprehension lit his face. His hand slid to her stomach. "Of course. I understand, sweetheart."

The feel of his big hand against her abdomen sent wild ripples of sensation through her. His child lay within, beyond the touch of his strength and warmth. Stacey's heart jumped. Could he possibly suspect . . . ? "What do you mean?" she asked warily.

His hand strayed over the curve of her hip and smoothed along the outside of her thigh. "It's *that* time of the month, hmm? Well, that certainly explains things."

The passion drained from her as if he had pulled some invisible plug. "Oh?"

"Your queasiness today, why Brynn made up that disjointed story about your being ill." He gave a little chuckle. "She needn't have bothered. I could have handled the straight facts. I'm thirty-nine years old, Stacey. I'm well acquainted with the facts of life."

Stacey stiffened, glaring at him. "Oh, are you?"

"And agreeing to go out with Cord Marshall and appear on his show clinches it. Your erratic behavior has a biological reason. Hormones." He seemed quite pleased to have worked it all out.

"Hormones," she repeated, struggling awkwardly to her feet. She longed to wipe the smug, masculine smile from his face. Hormones! "Get out of my apartment, you patronizing, condescending chauvinist!"

"Uh-oh." He smiled resignedly. "Stacey, I wasn't

being patronizing or condescending. And I'm not a chauvinist."

"Ha!" she snarled. "You're a chauvinist of the first order, Justin Marks!"

"Sweetheart, for heaven's sake—"

"Out!" She pointed to the door. "And *don't* call me sweetheart!"

He stood up and stared at her, his expression a mixture of exasperation, frustration—and, yes, amusement!

Stacey was outraged. "You insufferable macho clod! Get out!"

He adjusted his coat and straightened his tie. "I'm leaving, honey. There's no need to get so upset."

"I can't help myself. It's the hormones, remember?"

He chose to answer her seriously. "I understand, darling." He cupped the nape of her neck with his hand and kneaded it gently. "Why don't you take a couple of aspirins and go to bed with a nice hot-water bottle?"

"I could kill you for that!" she shouted, flinging his hand away from her.

He nodded. "And you might get off too. In England, several women have been acquitted of murder using the PMS syndrome as a defense."

Stacey felt as if she were going to explode. She could get angrier with Justin than with any living mortal on the face of the earth. And right now, his misguided male concern was more intolerable than his most officious command.

"Stacey, don't worry about being in the office by nine tomorrow." He paused by the door. "Come in at noon if you feel up to it, or spend the whole day at home if you like."

"In bed? With my hot-water bottle?"

He had already disappeared into the elevator by the time she gave the door a mighty slam.

Four

When the alarm went off at seven o'clock the next morning, Stacey shut it off, rolled over onto her stomach, buried her face in the pillow, and groaned. Had she slept at all last night? She had tossed and turned for hours, far too emotionally wired to fall asleep. She must've drunk at least two quarts of warm milk, but that age-old panacea had failed to induce drowsiness.

The temptation to remain in bed was exceedingly strong. Knowing that she wasn't expected to appear at her father's office until noon, if at all, heightened the temptation to stay abed. But it also strengthened her resolve to be in that office *before* nine A.M. as well! She flung back the covers and determinedly climbed out of bed. "Take a nice hot-water bottle to bed," he'd said. "Spend the whole day in bed if you like." Stacey bristled with a resurgence of anger from the night before. She had promised herself, as she'd seethed in the living room for an hour after Justin's departure, that she wouldn't accept a crumb of his chauvinistic male sympathy.

Naturally, today was the day that every one of her skirts were too tight at the waist and all her slacks were unzippable. Had she grown bigger overnight or had her final acknowledgment of her pregnancy permitted her to stop squeezing herself into ill-fitting, uncomfortable clothes? she wondered. She surveyed the contents of her wardrobe and realized that she literally had nothing to wear.

"Brynn!" she called in desperation. "Help!"

Brynn was two and a half inches taller than Stacey and a whole dress size larger. Her red-and-black-striped minidress wasn't quite so mini on Stacey, but at least it was a roomy, comfortable fit. She wore black tights and low-heeled red sling-back shoes, and borrowed Brynn's black-and-red, geometric-design earrings and pendant. Her light brown hair swung around her face in its thick, blunt cut and her long bangs accented her eyes becomingly.

"How do I look?" she asked Brynn. She hadn't felt this nervous dressing for an occasion since her senior prom!

Brynn surveyed her and smiled dryly. "You look great for Nick Erlich's office. But don't they all dress for success in your dad's territory, Stace? Have you ever seen a member of his staff in anything but a blue or a gray suit?"

"And a white shirt," Stacey added glumly. "No, I haven't."

"And the red shoes will put them into orbit. Aren't orthopedic oxfords the order of the day over there? Even for the young?"

"Brynn, I'm never going to fit in. There isn't even a job for me, not a real one. Only this stupid position that Justin created to—to—"

"Keep you near him?" Brynn suggested.

"Keep me under surveillance," amended Stacey. "What he'd really like to do is to lock my brothers and me up in some inaccessible dungeon with a moat surrounding it. The thought of us regularly facing the national press is enough to make him break out in hives." She reached into the closet for her raincoat. It was raining yet again. Had they even *seen* the sun for the past two weeks? "Well, I'm off."

"So early?" Brynn glanced at her watch. "Stacey, it's not even eight o'clock yet. If you leave now, you'll be there before eight-twenty, and our hours are nine to five. Remember?"

"Dad's zealous staff gets there earlier. And if I'm stuck there, I might as well *try* to be a part of the team."

"But you should eat something," Brynn said insistently. "In your condition, you should eat a hearty breakfast. I'll fix it for you."

Stacey's already queasy stomach rebelled at the thought. "Brynnie, I'd rather skydive without a parachute than face a meal right now."

"Sounds like Baby X is making his presence felt."

"Most definitely." She was beginning to feel more acutely nauseated the longer she was up and about.

"Meet you for lunch?" Brynn asked, and Stacey suppressed a shudder. Even the thought of food was revolting right now. "I'll give you a call if I can," she promised tentatively.

Stacey drove the short distance to Capitol Hill, feeling worse by the minute. When she arrived at her father's large office suite, she suppressed the urge to sink onto the sofa in the reception area and lay her head down. Diana Drew, the receptionist, cast a speaking glance at Stacey's attire and pursed her lips, but made no comment.

"Your desk is in Justin's office," she told Stacey. "But Justin said you wouldn't be in today."

"Oh, I'm full of surprises," Stacey said, making a valiant attempt at amiability. Diana did not respond. "Quite" was all she said with the thinnest of smiles.

Stacey suppressed a sigh. It was no use trying to be friendly with Diana. She might idolize her senator-boss, but her warmth for him didn't extend to his family. Every attractive politician had at least one Diana-type on his staff—women who completely subordinated their own lives to their idols'. None of the other men they met could compare to their mythical hero, and they dedicated themselves to living in the shadows of their glamorous bosses. Political groupies, Sterne called them, and he tried to use his relationship with the senator to score with them. It very seldom worked. Stacey knew her father had quite a few such admirers. She'd seen the glow in these women's eyes when they looked at or spoke to Bradford Lipton. Did her father ever physically reciprocate their devotion? she wondered, not for the first time. It was a question that sometimes troubled her, and one which she really didn't want answered. She feared the answer.

"Is Justin here yet?" she asked Diana conversationally.

"Of course. He's in his office," Diana replied in those same cool tones.

Shrugging, Stacey made her way to Justin's office, fighting the miserable queasiness and nervous unease. She'd deliberately neglected to tell Brynn about Justin's visit the night before, but she had spent most of the night reliving those hot kisses on the sofa. Her legs were shaking as she reached Justin's door.

"You'd better knock first, Stacey," said Frederick Rhodes, her father's legislative assistant, who was passing by. Like all of the senator's staff, he tended to regard Stacey and her brothers as harebrained liabilities. "Justin had some important calls to make and he's probably still on the phone."

"I always knock before entering, Freddie," Stacey said sweetly. "It's a little lesson I learned at my mother's knee." Fred was looking askance at her outfit and he was *not* pleased she had called him Freddie. Stacey's smile grew even sweeter. The staff was going to hate having her here as much as she was going to hate being here. She knocked at the door and Justin called out, "Who is it?"

"Me."

There was a momentary wait and then Justin himself opened the door. "Stacey? But I thought you weren't coming in today. And certainly not before eight-thirty." He was wearing a tailored charcoal-gray suit and a stiffly starched white shirt. The inevitable dark blue tie hung straight and proper. His usual uniform.

"I'm full of surprises," she said, trying out the line that had failed with Diana Drew. It drew a wide smile from Justin. "You certainly are. Come in, Stacey."

She was startled by the warmth of his greeting. He took her arm and guided her into his office. He seemed so glad to see her, she thought wonderingly. "Your desk has been installed." He pointed to the small metal desk tucked into the corner of his office. A telephone and an empty metal basket sat on the desk top.

"I see." She sank gratefully into the government-issue vinyl chair. "And exactly what am I supposed to do at this desk, other than make frequent trips to the water cooler?"

"Oh, we'll find something for you to do." Justin was still smiling, Stacey noted through a dizzying haze of nausea. She couldn't ever remember him smiling so much.

"In fact, right now you could go to the cafeteria

and bring me back a blueberry Danish and a large glass of tomato juice."

Her stomach turned upside down. Gooey blueberries on sticky, sweet pastry and thick red juice. She shuddered, blanching at the image. And if she had to go to the cafeteria and smell the bacon and sausage sizzling on the grill, or even *look* at the eggs, she would die, right there in the food line.

"I had an interesting job with Nick Erlich, Justin," she said, somewhat weakly. She was feeling so sick, maybe she would die right then and there. "I sorted, read, and answered the letters from his constituents in his home district. Have you demoted me to a—a waitress for the Lipton staff?"

"Of course not, Stacey. Your job here will be extremely interesting. But right now—Stacey? Stacey, are you all right?"

She was not all right. He had no sooner asked the question when she became dreadfully sick, right in the trash can! Justin moved quickly to hold her head. When the spasm was finally finished, he mopped the icy perspiration from her face with his large white handkerchief. Stacey was totally mortified.

"You're going to see a doctor," he said. His face was set in grim lines. "And you're going to stay in bed and do whatever else he tells you until you're completely well again."

If he only knew! "No!" she said, realizing she was close to tears. "I'm all right, Justin. Honestly!"

He frowned and picked up the phone. "Kay, get me Dr. Simpson," he barked into the receiver. Victor Simpson was the senator's personal physician, and a well-known internist at the army's Walter Reed Hospital in another section of the city. After a few minutes' conversation, Justin hung up the phone. "The doctor will see you. Get your coat, Stacey. I'm taking you there now."

"No, you can't! You have too much to do today, Justin. You can't waste time sitting around a doctor's office."

"I'm taking you to the doctor's office, Stacey," he said flatly in a tone that brooked no argument.

Nevertheless, Stacey argued. "Justin, this is absurd. I'm perfectly all right and even if I weren't, I don't need *you* to take me to the doctor's."

"I'm taking you, Stacey." He handed her her coat and purse at the moment the phone began to ring.

Stacey grabbed the receiver, desperate for a diversion. A moment later she handed Justin the phone. "It's CBS News. They want Dad to make an appearance on their morning news program," she whispered.

Justin took the call, of course. He couldn't brush off such an important publicity source as CBS News. Stacey snatched her coat and purse and ran out of his office. "Stacey!" she heard Justin call after her. "Stacey, come back here!"

But he didn't follow her. He couldn't. Stacey knew she was safe. She gave a mental thanks to CBS and their timely phone call. An appearance on the morning news show was precisely the sort of coveted exposure any candidate craved. No campaign manager would pass up the opportunity to arrange such a coup.

Stacey drove her bright blue BMW directly to her parents' spacious colonial-style home in Chevy Chase. Justin Marks would no doubt expect her to return to her own apartment, so she could safely escape him in the sanctity of the senator's house.

Caroline Lipton was on her way to a charity committee board meeting, looking feminine and lovely in a tailored, oatmeal-colored suit. "That's an—er—interesting dress, Stacey," she said tactfully. "Are you on your way to a disco, dear?"

Stacey had to smile. Her always carefully dressed mother would shudder if she thought her daughter had dressed this way for work! "No, Mother. Actually, I'm still feeling a little—um—under the weather. I thought I'd take you up on your offer of my old room and Grace's chicken soup."

"Wonderful, dear. I'll tell Grace." Caroline touched her daughter's forehead. "You're flushed, but not feverish. My poor Stacey. I wish I didn't have to rush off and leave you."

Stacey wanted to press her mother's palm to her cheek and savor her touch, to beg her to stay with her. But, of course, she didn't. Only Spencer had challenged the foundation of the cool Lipton family reserve and married an openly warm and affectionate woman. And his wife Patty made the senator and his wife uncomfortable, Stacey knew. All that touching, all that kissing. They didn't quite approve.

But the tradition of family reserve worked to Stacey's advantage in this case. Her mother would not press her for information and her privacy would be unquestioningly honored. "Mother, I'd like to rest and I really don't want to be disturbed. Would you ask Grace to tell anyone who might call for me that I'm not here? Unless it's Brynn, of course."

"Yes, I'll tell her, dear. You go upstairs and rest."

Stacey climbed into bed and slept past one. When she got up this time, she was no longer nauseated but ravenously hungry. She ate two big bowls of chicken soup and three of the biscuits the housekeeper had baked especially for her.

"That was wonderful, Grace." Replete, Stacey leaned back in her chair at the kitchen table. "I feel a million times better."

"Good." Grace carried the dishes to the sink. "Now maybe you'll call Justin Marks and tell him where you are."

Stacey froze. "H-He called?"

"Four times. Oh, I followed your mother's instructions," Grace said dryly as she stacked the dishes in the dishwasher. "But I don't think she suspected that Justin Marks would be calling, did she? Why are you really here, Stacey Lynn? What have you gotten yourself into now?"

The senior Liptons might respect their children's privacy, but not Grace, not if she suspected something was amiss. And her suspicions were seldom wrong. Amazing Grace, the Lipton children used to call Grace McKellum, who'd joined the household shortly after Sterne's birth. Grace had known the senator's first wife, Dorothy, who had died tragically in a hotel fire. Grace had taken care of young Spencer and Sterne until their father's marriage to twenty-one-year-old Caroline Courtney. She'd been there when the young bride had had had to cope with the problems of becoming an instant mother to the two boys, then aged four and six. And she had known Stacey since her newborn-baby days and could, as she often informed Stacey, "read her like a book."

But as much as Stacey might long to, this time she couldn't unload her problem on Grace. The housekeeper would feel honor-bound to tell the senior Liptons. Stacey knew her primary loyalty was invariably to them. "Oh, you know Justin, Grace," she said blithely. "He's always on my case about something."

"I know that you torment the poor man unmercifully and always have, miss. Is this another attempt to drive that poor soul around the bend?"

"You've got it backward, Grace. He torments me!"

"Stacey Lynn Lipton, you've been teasing Justin Marks for years! I remember you at age sixteen, in your high-school kilt and knee socks, waltzing by him and tossing off some outrageous remark guaranteed to make his hair stand on end. And nothing has changed that I can see."

"Not true!" Stacey sniffed indignantly. "I don't know why you're taking *his* side, Grace."

"I'm not taking anyone's side, Stacey. But you're up to something, I know you are."

If only it were as simple as that, Stacey thought wistfully. Grace would be stunned if she were aware of the seriousness of the problem. For just a moment, Stacey wished she were still a schoolgirl dreaming up some scheme to drive Justin crazy. Now she was carrying his child, and she'd never felt so confused and afraid in her entire life.

The telephone began to ring. Stacey swallowed. "Grace, if it's him . . ."

"I know, I know," Grace said as she started for the phone in the hall. "I'll follow your mother's instructions to the letter, although I want you to know that I don't approve." Moments later, she called Stacey to the phone. "It's Brynn. Your mother said you were in to her."

Stacey heaved a sigh of relief. "Of course." She took the phone. "Hi, Brynnie!"

"Grace, are you sure you don't know where Stacey is?" came Brynn's voice, sounding tense and unnatural. She pronounced each word slowly and carefully. "Justin Marks is *right here* and he is quite concerned that Stacey didn't keep her doctor's appointment."

Stacey gasped. "Oh! Brynn, thanks!" Brynn had obviously divined that she didn't want Justin Marks to know her whereabouts. The remark about the doctor's appointment had no doubt been the tip-off. Stacey quickly passed the phone to

Grace. "Justin is right there with Brynn, Grace. Tell him that—"

"Tell Grace not to bother telling me anything," Justin's voice boomed over the line. "I'll be at the house to pick you up within the hour, Stacey. And don't even dream of trying to disappear again." There was the harsh sound of the receiver being forcefully replaced in its cradle.

"He heard." Stacey groaned. "He must have been holding the phone for Brynn. He's such a bully!"

"Justin Marks is a very determined man, Stacey, you've always known that," Grace reminded her. "And he knows you very well."

Very well, indeed, Stacey thought gloomily.

Justin's expression was hard and unsmiling when he arrived at the door of Senator Lipton's home thirty-eight minutes later. He didn't respond to Grace's greetings, and Stacey knew he was angry with the housekeeper. She'd lied to him four times and Justin Marks did not take kindly to being thwarted.

Stacey descended the staircase in what she hoped was a loftily regal manner. At least she didn't feel weak or sick anymore. Her color was good and her tawny-gold eyes were alert with challenge. "Hello, Justin," she said coolly. Damn, she thought. His suit, shirt, and tie didn't have a wrinkle, while she'd slept in Brynn's dress. She felt at a distinct disadvantage and tilted her chin higher. "I want you to know that I deeply resent your overbearing, autocratic interference in my life."

"So what else is new?" he snapped. "And it's no use stalling, Stacey. Let's go."

"You behave yourself now, Stacey," Grace admonished her as they went out the door.

Stacey grimaced. Justin scowled. "That'll be the

day," he muttered. He stuffed her into his stolid gray—but of course—Oldsmobile. He was remote and cold, the Justin Marks she knew so well. She thought of the pleased warmth with which he'd greeted her that morning at the office and felt an odd lump form in her throat. This icily controlled Justin seemed incapable of smiles or warmth of any kind.

They didn't speak at all during the drive to Walter Reed Hospital through the dense Beltway traffic. Stacey knew Justin was furious with her. What she didn't understand was why he was wasting his precious time driving her across town to a doctor's appointment.

He must consider it a power struggle between them, she decided at last. And he was determined to emerge the victor. Her mouth tightened and she concentrated on her plan of action. She had thought of a way to deal with the doctor, after all. . . .

Justin Marks had to stay in the waiting room of Dr. Simpson's office, a fact that obviously irritated him. He would've preferred to have barged into the examining room, where Stacey was sitting on a paper-covered table wearing her panties and a short cotton smock.

"Dr. Simpson, don't doctors take some sort of oath upon graduating from medical school?" she asked as the doctor checked her blood pressure.

"Yes," he said. "It's called the Hippocratic oath, and in it the physician pledges not to reveal confidential information about his patients." He checked her pulse.

"Did you take it, Dr. Simpson? The oath, I mean."

"Oh, yes."

"Then I'm going to hold you to it, Dr. Simpson."

She faced him squarely. "You see, I'm going to have a baby and . . ."

Twenty minutes later, Stacey and Victor Simpson emerged from the office into the waiting room. Justin dropped the magazine he had been leafing through and rose to his feet. "Well?" he asked impatiently, his ebony eyes fastened on Stacey.

"A perfectly healthy young woman," Dr. Simpson said heartily. Stacey flashed Justin an I-told-you-so smile.

"She's really all right?" His gaze swept Stacey from head to toe.

"Yes, indeed." The doctor turned to Stacey. "And you won't forget what you promised me, Stacey?"

"I won't forget," she said. Inside her purse were prescriptions for prenatal vitamins and iron, plus something to help control her nausea. And he'd made her promise to see an obstetrician within the next week, giving her the names of some trusted colleagues.

"Well, I'm glad there isn't anything wrong with you," Justin said as he and Stacey walked to the elevators. "I was beginning to think . . . Why on earth did you have to run away, Stacey?" He sighed with exasperation.

"I was put on this earth for the sole purpose of irritating you, Justin," she said dryly. "I was just doing my job."

"The things you say!" The corners of his mouth curved into a reluctant smile. "What did you promise the doctor, Stacey?"

Lord, he was thorough! she thought. He never missed a thing, nor did he ever fail to follow up on the smallest detail. She chewed her lower lip. "I—uh—I promised I'd give Dr. Simpson a plug on *The Cord Marshall Show* on Saturday. Maybe he needs the business."

"Stacey!"

"Oh, all right! I promised I'd send him some autographed pictures of Dad," she said, pleased with her quick thinking.

Justin accepted the lie with a satisfied nod. "That can certainly be arranged. I'll have June mail him five tomorrow. Or did he ask for more?"

"I think five autographed pictures of Dad will be a nice surprise for the doctor, Justin."

"I'll include some campaign literature and some buttons too. Simpson can pass them around to his friends. It never hurts to have as many physicians . . ."

Stacey deliberately tuned Justin out as he went on to discuss the possibility of winning the AMA endorsement. She always tuned him out when he started to sound like he was being interviewed on *Good Morning America*. As they left the hospital, she realized he was still talking.

"The beauty of an early November announcement is that it gives the candidate time to perfect his style and tighten up his campaign in the early days. By spring, we'll be in top form. . . ."

Stacey grimaced. Had she *really* spent an explosively impassioned night with this man? In his boring, drab clothes, spouting political strategy in that impersonally serious way of his, he seemed as inaccessible and emotionless as an IBM computer. Was there really a sensitive and passionate man trapped inside that gray-suited automaton? The dichotomy between the two was mind-boggling.

"Agreed, Stacey?" Justin asked as they reached the car.

"What?" She stared at him blankly.

"I suggested your spending most of February in New Hampshire campaigning for your father in the primary," he said with a hint of impatience in his voice.

In February she would be in her seventh month of pregnancy. She sucked in her cheeks. "I thought you had the New Hampshire primary sewn up. Your canvassers, your great advance team, your well-oiled organization."

He gazed down at her with an ill-concealed mixture of exasperation and frustration. "We've laid the groundwork with impeccable thoroughness, but we can't leave it at that. The campaign itself must be handled with the same attention to detail. We're leaving nothing to chance, and I expect everyone in your family to pitch in and cooperate to the utmost."

In February, the month of the first state primary, she would be seven months pregnant! "I think I'll be doing the campaign a big favor by keeping a low profile, Justin." She climbed into his gray Olds and closed the door. She'd be doing the campaign an even greater favor if she disappeared for a few years.

When he climbed behind the steering wheel, Justin was scowling. "You're determined to be difficult about this, aren't you, Stacey?"

She leaned her head against the head rest and closed her eyes. They were on two totally opposite tracks. His mind was filled with the upcoming campaign while her thoughts centered on their secret child. Who would have to remain a secret for a long time. There was no way she could bring herself to confide in this politically obsessed man.

"Why do you care so much, Justin?" she found herself asking. She was suddenly curious about him, wanted to know what motivated him. "I know that running for president is the ultimate ego trip for my father, but you're strictly a behind-the-scenes man. What's in all this for you except a killing schedule and pressure and exhaustion and repetition?"

"That's your idea of the political process? That's the way you view a presidential campaign?" Justin sounded incredulous. "As an ego trip? As exhaustion and anxiety and pressure?"

Stacey nodded, a gleam in her eyes. "Did I forget to mention dehumanizing and hypocritical? Add those to the list."

He stared at her, shocked. "How can you be so negative? Stacey, it's the opportunity of a lifetime! It's a chance to implement the senator's views—which happen to be my own, as well—into viable programs for the stabilization and betterment of our society, to shore up the free world's—"

"Justin, this isn't *Meet the Press*. Can you tell me, minus the rhetoric, why you're willing to dedicate your life to making my father president? I'm curious. I'd really like to know."

"What makes me tick?" He smiled slightly.

"You're a complete enigma to me, Justin. I've known you for ten years, but you've remained an unfathomable stranger."

An odd look shadowed his face. He put the car in gear and steered it into the steady stream of traffic. "Have you ever read any of your father's economic proposals or foreign policy statements?" he asked. Stacey shook her head no. The man was obviously incapable of conversing without political rherotic, she thought sadly.

"Well," he continued, "those proposals, those ideas and opinions, are mine, Stacey. Formulated and written by me. Oh, your father chooses his stands on the headline-grabbing family and morality issues, but I've been the one to create his economic and foreign policy positions."

Stacey shrugged. "I think I'm missing your point, Justin."

"Economics was my major at Stanford," he went on as if she hadn't spoken. "And after I received my

MBA at the Wharton School of Finance, I tried my hand in the business world. I did well financially and learned a lot of cutthroat strategies, but ultimately I was bored. I liked the world of ideas. I was thinking of accepting a university teaching position when I met your father at a fund-raiser in New York City. He interested me. He wanted national stature, but he didn't have the depth and the creative force to achieve it. From my marketing and advertising experience, I knew all about trends and images and how to sell a product. Your father asked me to join his staff on that basis alone. But it was as his administrative assistant that I was given free rein to put together an economic policy based on my pet theories and ideas." His eyes shone with enthusiasm. "And when we needed a foreign policy stance, I devoured everything I could on the subject, I spoke to experts in the field, I took courses. It was an exhilarating experience— learning, formulating and shaping ideas."

"But you do all the work and Dad takes all the credit!" Stacey protested. "Everyone thinks those ideas are his. Don't you mind, Justin?"

"Of course not. I'm not a politician, Stacey. My marketing skills aside, I'm an economist and a foreign policy buff. Running the campaign is just a temporary thing, a necessity to get your father elected. I don't have the charisma or the money or the political ties that your father does. He is the candidate—the conduit, if you wish—of my ideas. The senator and I both recognize our value to each other. We have a smooth, harmonious working relationship."

"And if he reaches the White House, you'll be his confidante and hold an important, high-ranking position. You'll be a man of great power." It was beginning to make sense to Stacey now. Depressing sense.

"Yes," Justin admitted frankly. "And I won't deny that power is quite alluring, but there is more to it than that. There's a feeling of belonging. . . ." His voice trailed off and he frowned, as if he had revealed too much.

He didn't want to pursue the topic, that was clear, but Stacey pressed on. "Belonging to what, Justin?"

"It's irrelevant." He gave a slightly sheepish smile. "I don't want to bore you."

He was clearly ill at ease. Stacey was fascinated. There was no way she could let the subject drop now. "You've been boring me for years with all your political jargon and it never bothered you. Tell me, Justin."

"Tell you what?" he hedged.

"What you don't want to tell me. Something about a feeling of belonging."

"Stacey, I don't care to discuss it."

She moved toward the middle of the seat, closer to him. "You know I'll never stop badgering you until you tell me, Justin." She watched the muscles of his jaw tense, saw him tighten his fingers around the steering wheel. She moved closer. "Go on, Justin," she said softly. She was teasing him, she realized, and Grace's accusation rang in her ears. "You've been teasing that man for years." Had she? It was an unsettling thought.

Justin drew a deep breath. "I've never belonged to anything or anyone," he said flatly, his voice impassive. "I was raised in a series of foster homes, never a part of the real family, although they were kind enough to me, I suppose. I knew the only thing I had going for me was my intelligence, so I studied and worked to the exclusion of everything else—friends, sports, social activities. I won a scholarship to Stanford and continued the pattern. I was an honor student, but never a part of campus life. The same held true for graduate school and all through my career."

"And by having power, you don't really have to belong," Stacey said thoughtfully. "You're in by default. You control." She stared at him. This was the first time he had ever shared such personal information. She'd had no idea of his lonely and loveless early years. She had never bothered to learn anything personal about him, she realized somewhat ashamedly.

He shrugged, clearly uncomfortable. She was certain that he was regretting his momentary lapse into the personal realm. But Stacey wanted to know more. She felt an oddly compelling drive to delve into the private life of Justin Marks.

"Haven't you ever wanted something beyond professional or academic success? A—a family of your own, perhaps?" What on earth had made her ask *that*? The question had slipped out, to her own disconcertion.

"I suppose I'd have experienced the pull for family ties at some point," Justin conceded with a half-smile. "But ten years ago I came to work for your father and became very well acquainted with the Lipton family and—"

"Say no more," Stacey interjected dryly. "Observing the Liptons at close range effectively killed all desires for a family of your own. That's not surprising. We are a strange bunch."

"I didn't mean that, Stacey. I meant that once I was involved with your family, I felt a part of it. I felt like I had a family of my own."

She gaped at him. Justin Marks felt a part of her family? she thought with amazement. The notion was incredible. Never once in the ten years since they'd known him had any of the Liptons considered him a part of the family. Not even her parents. Justin Marks might be an invaluable AA, but he wasn't one of them. And all this time he had thought that his peripheral relationship with the Liptons was what belonging to a family was like. But then, how could he know any differently? He'd never belonged to any family. He thought his only worthwhile quality was his intelligence. She stared at the handsome man beside her and was blinded by a sudden rush of tears. Those infernal hormones again! She had the most horrifying urge to weep over Justin Marks's lonely past and sad misapprehensions. She fumbled in her purse for a tissue.

"Will you have dinner with me tonight?" he asked, and she was grateful that the Beltway traffic and the rain was forcing him to keep his attention strictly on the road. She couldn't have explained her tears to him. She couldn't explain them to herself!

"I don't think that would be a very good idea, Justin," she murmured. Not when she was so vulnerably attuned to him.

"Why not? We both have to eat, don't we?" he asked ingenuously.

"But not together."

"Yes," he said firmly. "Together, Stacey."

"Justin, it—it just won't work." She crumpled the tissue and stuffed it into her bag. "We're too different. And I don't indulge in casual affairs."

"I know you don't," he said in an oddly satisfied tone. "And what's between us is far from casual, Stacey."

How on earth was she supposed to answer that one? she wondered. He was right, of course. Whatever the feelings between them were, they weren't casual. The intensity between them had always been fierce. She stared out the window at the drizzling rain, then felt compelled to ask, "Do you have—er—casual affairs, Justin?"

In all the years she had known him, she'd never seen him with a date, she realized with a start. He was always in the background with his statistical data, engineering the senator and his family this way and that. But those times—at her father's office, at political events, or at strategy meetings at the Lipton houses—weren't social occasions. Justin Marks had been present in his professional capacity, in his eternal gray suit and white shirt. The Liptons didn't socialize with the senator's AA. Stacey found herself wondering what sort of woman appealed to Justin. What if he had appeared at some Lipton-related event with a beautiful blonde in tow? She felt a peculiar churning in her stomach that was entirely unrelated to Baby X's presence.

Justin was clearly uncomfortable with the subject. "There have been a few women over the years." He shrugged. "But nothing that lasted. There were no commitments."

She refused to speculate on why his answer so delighted her. "Because you're totally dedicated to your career?"

"Maybe I was waiting for you to grow up and notice me, Stacey," he countered lightly.

"And if I believe that, you'll try to sell me beachfront property in Iowa."

He cast her a quick and undecipherable sidelong glance. "If we've dispensed with that topic, can we go back to the subject of dinner tonight? The dinner we're having together?"

"You're very persistent," she said irritably.

"I certainly am. Persistence is the hallmark of anyone in politics. Now, where shall we eat?"

She heaved an exasperated sigh. He obviously wasn't going to accept graciously her refusal. And she was too tired to keep sparring with him. "Oh, all right," she grumbled with ill grace. "I'll have dinner with you. But that's all, Justin! I'm not going to bed with you," she added fiercely, her cheeks warm.

Justin made no reply. But Stacey didn't miss the pleased little smile that lit his face. And though she tried hard to work up a protective anger, it was no use. She wasn't angry with Justin Marks for his insistence that she have dinner with him, nor for the high-handed way he had spirited her to the doctor. And that smile on his face touched her in a way that she didn't dare define.

Five

"Could we stop at a drugstore?" Stacey asked as they exited from the Beltway onto the divided highway leading into the District. "Dr. Simpson gave me prescriptions for vitamins and iron that I'd like to have filled." She didn't mention the anti-nausea medicine, which she deemed an absolute necessity.

"Of course. I don't mind stopping. If the doctor prescribed them for you, he must want you to begin taking them right away."

Stacey hid a smile. When applied in her favor, Justin's maddeningly careful attention to detail was not so maddening at all.

It was drizzling as Justin pulled the Olds into the parking lot of a drugstore that was large enough to resemble a supermarket. He got out of the car, and Stacey pulled the belt of her raincoat around her and reached for the door handle. The door seemed to be stuck and she gave it a forceful shove with her shoulder. It flung open at the same instant Justin approached it.

She'd never dreamed he would come around to her side to open the door for her. When was the last time a man had performed *that* little courtesy for her? In these liberated times, women were supposed to fend heartily for themselves. And Stacey—

accustomed to fending heartily for herself—had sent the door swinging open just in time to crack Justin right in the middle of his forehead!

There was a sickening thud and blood began to spurt from the cut on his forehead almost instantly. Stacey screamed and jumped out of the car. Justin stared straight ahead, glassy-eyed, as his knees began to buckle. She watched in frozen horror as he crumpled to a heap in the parking lot.

"Oh, my God, Justin!" she cried as she knelt beside him. "I've killed you!"

He opened one eye and gingerly raised a hand to his forehead. "I feel as if I've been run over by the University of Nebraska defensive line," he murmured with a wry smile.

"Oh, Justin!" Although his lapse of unconsciousness had lasted only seconds, Stacey had been more afraid than she'd ever been in her entire life. A purple bruise was already beginning to form on his forehead and blood was pouring from an ugly gash in the middle of it. "Justin, I'm so sorry!" she said as tears ran down her face. "I didn't know you were there. I never expected you to open the door for me. Oh!" She cradled his head on her lap and fumbled through her purse for something to press against the bleeding wound. "I've used my last tissue. What can I use to stop the bleeding? Oh, Justin, I'm so terribly sorry!"

"It wasn't your fault, Stacey. Accidents happen," he said soothingly, and the irony of the situation wasn't lost on Stacey. She'd split open his forehead and now *he* was attempting to comfort *her*. "I have a handkerchief in the pocket of my coat," he added.

She found the square white handkerchief neatly folded in the inner pocket of his suit coat. She pressed it against the cut, gazing down at him with concern. Justin wasn't his usual polished and immaculate self now. His clothes were wet from the rain, grimy from the gravel of the parking lot, and bloody from his cut. His hair was tousled and damp. The sight of him lying there, so mussed and un-Justinlike, brought a fresh torrent of tears to Stacey's eyes. He seemed so vulnerable, all dirtied and bloodied and hurt. And it was all her fault.

She pressed the handkerchief more firmly against the cut and he winced. "I'm sorry!" she wailed. "Poor Justin!"

"I'm all right," he assured her. "But I feel a bit foolish lying out here in the rain." He stood up abruptly and took a few staggering steps before he stumbled. Stacey ran to him and grabbed him, supporting him with both arms.

"Are you dizzy? Lean on me, Justin. I think you got up too quickly." She was alarmed by his color, a chalky white. "You probably have a concussion." Actually, she was sure he did. The door had hit him hard and his momentary loss of consciousness and subsequent dizziness confirmed it to her. Lucas had been concussed several times in his violent football career and she was familiar with the symptoms.

Leaning against Stacey, Justin eased himself into the car, holding the handkerchief to his head. It was already soaked with blood. "Give me your keys, Justin," she said. "I'm driving you to the nearest hospital." Her hands shook as she searched his pockets for his keys.

He rested his hands on her hips as she stood above him. "Hospital? There's no need, Stacey. I'll just pour a little iodine on the cut when I get home and—"

"We're going to the hospital, Justin." She had his keys in her hands. "That cut needs stitches and you have a concussion."

He protested the whole way to the hospital and

Stacey ignored his every protest. "Stop trying to be brave, Justin. I know you're suffering. Please don't feel you have to put on a front with me."

She helped him out of the car and into the emergency room, confronting the nurse on duty with the fierceness of a mother lion protecting her cub. Stacey knew how to play senator's daughter when the occasion demanded. In spite of her wet and bloody clothes, she stated her name, her father's name, and insisted that Justin be seen at once. He was.

She stayed with him throughout the examination of the cut, the X rays, and the four stitches required to close the wound. The doctor agreed with Stacey's diagnosis: Justin did indeed have a concussion and should rest quietly for the next few days. He also prescribed pain medication for the headaches that might follow.

"A few days of rest and quiet!" Justin said wryly as they left the hospital. He had an impressive bandage on his forehead and Stacey kept her arm firmly around his waist for support. "If that doctor saw my schedule for the next few days, he'd know what an impossible order that was."

"Justin, you have to listen to the doctor. You can't rush into your usual hypermanic schedule after an injury like this!"

"Stacey, I'm fine. I can't lie around for days just because I bumped my head."

They had reached the Olds, and Stacey insisted on helping Justin into it. "You're going straight home to bed, Justin. And you're going to follow the doctor's orders. I'm going to make sure that you do."

His lips quirked in amusement. "You're very determined, Stacey."

"Persistence is the hallmark of anyone in politics," she said, quoting his own words back to him. "Even for those unwilling ones on the periphery."

They stopped at a drugstore to pick up Justin's pain pills, and to have Stacey's prescriptions filled also. She was going to need that antinausea medication if she was to take proper care of Justin. "I think I'll stay in the car this time," he remarked dryly as she pulled into the parking lot. He smiled as he spoke and Stacey stared at him with increasing admiration. He had been so brave and so congenial at the hospital. She'd never realized what a droll sense of humor he had. And to be able to make jokes at a time like this, when he must be half delirious with pain . . . Impulsively, she reached over to give his arm a squeeze. "I'll be right back with the medicine, Justin," she told him warmly.

Twenty minutes later Justin directed her to his apartment, which consisted of several rooms on the second floor of a renovated house near the Capitol. The walls were painted white, there were old-style venetian blinds instead of curtains at the windows, and the furniture was a hodge-podge of outdated pieces that were surely rejects, even in their own time.

"Oh!" Stacey glanced around the appalling living room. "What an eclectic decor! Did you—er—decorate your apartment yourself, Justin?"

"No. I rented it already furnished."

She breathed a sigh of relief. "Then you won't take offense if I say that the furniture is absolutely hideous? The print on that sofa is an eyesore! When were gargantuan orange roses on a sickly pink background ever fashionable? And to put a mustard-and-blue-striped chair next to it is criminal!"

Justin laughed. "I really don't spend much time here. It's convenient to the office and since I didn't have any furniture of my own . . ." He shrugged laconically.

The kitchen and the bedroom reflected the same dreary and impersonal decor. There was nothing of Justin Marks, the man, in this place. "You've lived here ten years?" Stacey asked incredulously. How had he endured it? And how could anyone live anywhere for ten years and not personalize the place in some little way?

"I bought a new mattress three years ago," Justin said, and sat down on the edge of the double bed. A brown corduroy spread covered it.

"That's good, because you're going to be spending the next few days in bed. Starting now." She turned to face him squarely. "While you're getting undressed, I'll fix you some dinner."

Before he could reply, she strode from the bedroom into the small, ugly kitchen. There was nothing in the refrigerator but a half-empty container of margarine. She scanned the cabinets affixed to the walls. They contained a mismatched assortment of plates and glasses that obviously came with the kitchen, a loaf of bread, and a large jar of instant hot chocolate. She marched back into Justin's bedroom, aghast. "There's no food here!"

He was still sitting on the edge of the bed. "I seldom eat here. Occasionally I'll have toast and hot chocolate in the morning. And the few times I come back here for dinner, I stop at a store and pick up something frozen."

"But you can't have a home without food!" Stacey exclaimed. She couldn't fathom it. Maybe Justin Marks really was some kind of computerized android!

He took off his suit coat and his tie, and as she watched him the thought struck her that Justin hadn't ever really had a home of his own, just as he'd never had a family of his own. Perhaps this dreary apartment with its dreadful furnishings and singular lack of staples was the closest he'd ever come to his own home, just as the Liptons were the closest he'd come to his own family. Both were depressingly far from the real thing.

He was watching her intently, as if trying to decipher her thoughts, then suddenly, he sank back onto the bed, one hand on his bandaged forehead.

"Justin!" She flew across the room to his side. "Are you having an attack of vertigo?" The doctor had warned of such a possibility.

"Uh—yes."

"Oh, poor Justin!" She carefully helped him ease his head onto the pillows. "Would you like one of your pain pills?" She unfastened the buttons of his shirt to permit him to breathe more easily. He caught her wrists and pressed her hands onto his chest. She felt the wiry dark hair and the strong, muscled warmth beneath her fingers and took a deep breath. At this moment Justin did not look like a man suffering from a serious blow to the head. He looked alert and intent and . . .

"Justin," she began, and tried to remove her hands. He held them firmly against his chest. "Have I ever told you how beautiful you are, Stacey?" he asked thickly.

Her heart gave a crazy little leap. But given the circumstances—the bed, the quiet, darkened room, the bandage on Justin's head!—common sense quickly asserted itself. She forced a light laugh. "You really are delirious, Justin. I look like something a cat wouldn't bother to drag in." She knew it was true. Her hair was damp and poker straight from the rain, and her dress was as wrinkled and bloody as his unfortunate gray suit. All traces of her makeup were long gone.

"No!" His hands left hers to cup her face. "No, Stacey, you're beautiful to me. Beautiful . . ." His husky voice was a caress in itself. One big hand slid to her neck and he brought her down to him with effortless strength. For one magic moment, she allowed herself to lie against him, her cheek pressed to the soft chest hair, feeling the muscled hardness of his body beneath her. One of his hands kneaded the nape of her neck and the other smoothed firmly over the curve of her hip. A small moan escaped from her lips as a lightning heat scorched through her.

With one swift movement, Justin thrust his leg between hers and flipped her over onto her back. He lay on his side beside her, his hand moving lightly over her, over her breasts and her stomach and her thighs. Her lips mouthed his name, but no sound came out as she stared into the dark, dark eyes so close to her own. And then slowly, inexorably, his mouth lowered to hers.

"Justin, no," she whispered. But it was only a token protest, she recognized that. She began to tremble. She wanted to feel his mouth on hers with an urgency that bordered on desperation.

His lips hovered above hers for just a moment. "Yes, Stacey." His hand eased between her thighs to caress her with possessive intimacy. "Yes, love."

She couldn't breathe, couldn't speak. Her lips parted on a sigh as she helplessly arched herself against his tantalizing fingers.

"You need me," he rasped out, watching her react to his touch. "You want me, Stacey. Tell me." He applied an exquisite, erotic pressure that sent her spinning headlong into sensual delirium. "Tell me, darling. I want to hear you say the words."

She was helpless to resist him, helpless to control the wild longing surging within her. His tongue sought hers lightly, teasingly, but she was denied the satisfying hardness of his mouth until she cried out, "Oh, Justin, I want you. I need you so!"

His mouth closed over hers and they kissed deeply, wildly, with a hungry heat that seemed to generate an even greater passion. His hand never ceased its dizzying, exciting caresses and Stacey clung to him, craving him, so close, so very close to . . .

The jarring ring of the telephone seemed to come from some other dimension, an offensive intruder upon their intensely private world. And it wouldn't stop! After six rings, they could no longer ignore it. The black phone perched on the nightstand continued to ring and ring until Justin moved away from Stacey with a curse and fumbled for the receiver.

"Hello?" he barked into the mouthpiece. "Yes, Fred. Yes, I did. Yes, I know. We released a statement that outlined . . ."

Political talk, Stacey thought. Something about a Senate vote count. She listened, unable to think or move or do anything at all. She felt weak and disoriented. It had been too rapid a descent from the heady peaks of sexual arousal. Now she lay on her back on the bed feeling empty and frustrated and increasingly angry. She saw Justin's eyes upon her and was suddenly aware of her position, sprawled on his bed, her legs wide apart, her breasts heaving from her shallow, erratic breathing. She sat up abruptly as a hot blush swept her from head to toe.

Justin's hand instantly snaked out to catch her arm. "Let me go!" she muttered fiercely under her breath. She resisted the urge to scream it aloud. Wouldn't Fred Rhodes on the other end of the line be stunned to know that the leader of the pack had the senator's daughter in his bedroom?

"Fred, I'll talk to you in the morning," Justin

said. He was holding her with forceful strength. She couldn't twist her arm free and the urge to holler grew stronger. Perhaps Justin realized it, for he instantly ended the call.

"Let go of my arm, Justin!" she roared the moment he severed the connection with Fred. "Now!"

"Sweetheart, I know you're upset," Justin said soothingly.

"You're damn right I'm upset! And if you don't let me go—"

"Lie down, darling. I know how close you were . . . Let me—"

"No!" Her whole body was ablaze with embarrassment. What had she done? Her loss of control was devastating, as alarming as it was infuriating. Stacey fought a horrifying desire to burst into tears. Her body was craving an emotional release. The pent-up sexual tension was boiling inside her. If he didn't let go of her . . .

He released his grip on her arm abruptly, and she scrambled from the bed and raced from the room. "I'm leaving!" she flung over her shoulder. Snatching her coat and purse from the atrocious striped chair in the living room, she marched to the door—and stopped dead. She didn't have her car! She would have to call a taxi to take her to her apartment.

Stacey gritted her teeth. Going back into Justin's bedroom to use his telephone was the last thing in the world she wanted to do at this point. But she had to get home and it was too far to walk. She would have to call a taxi and she would have to go into the bedroom to use the phone.

Squaring her shoulders, she entered the bedroom she had just fled. Her eyes widened at the sight of Justin lying flat on his back, his eyes closed. "Justin?" she called warily. He was very still. Her gaze rested on the bandage on his forehead and her heart gave a nervous jump. "Justin, are you all right?" She took a step closer to the bed.

He opened his eyes. "I thought you'd gone, Stacey."

"I have to call a taxi. My car is at my parents' house."

He raised a hand to his temple. "Would you like to take my car?" he asked in a voice so low she had to move closer to hear. She stood beside the bed, looking down at him, her pulses pounding.

"Justin, your head is hurting, isn't it?" Of course, it was! she thought. How could it not be? The doctor had prescribed rest and quiet, and the past half hour had held anything but! The man was injured, thanks to her, she berated herself, and she'd compounded his misery by totally ignoring the doctor's orders. "Justin," she whispered tentatively, daring to touch his thick black hair.

He closed his eyes and groaned. "You're in pain!" she cried in alarm.

He groaned again and rolled over onto his side. "Terribly." His voice was muffled. "Damn, I don't mean to complain, Stacey. I have no respect for self-pitying whiners."

"Oh, you're no such thing!" she exclaimed indignantly. "After all you've been through tonight . . . You've been wonderful, Justin."

He made a sound that she couldn't quite identify. Probably a moan of agony, she decided worriedly. The poor man! "Would you like one of your pain pills, Justin?"

"I'll take one later, after I've made myself some toast and hot chocolate for dinner. Go ahead and drive my car home, Stacey. The keys are—"

"Justin, I can't leave you at a time like this!" It

was unthinkable! To leave him alone and in pain in this horrid apartment without any food!

"Will you stay all night?" came the muffled voice.

She continued to stare down at him. Had anyone ever stayed with him when he was sick or in pain? she wondered, thinking of a lonely little boy who had grown up with no home or family of his own. Her heart contracted with pain for that child and her compassion went out to the political mastermind/workaholic who was lying so quietly on the bed. He was in pain and he needed her. She suddenly felt so close to him, as close as she'd felt during those intense and passionate times in his arms.

"Yes, Justin." The urge to touch him was overwhelming and she gave into it, running her hand lightly along the muscled length of his arm. "I'll stay with you."

They ordered a pizza from a nearby pizzeria that delivered. Justin was unalterably opposed to Stacey going grocery shopping alone at night, and it seemed easier to give in to him. She could stock his kitchen with food tomorrow, she assured herself.

They sat on the bed, the pizza box between them, and consumed the whole pie. Justin's injury hadn't seemed to interfere with his appetite. He ate five pieces of pizza and Stacey had three.

He had showered and changed into a pair of pale blue pajamas and she was unable to keep her eyes off him. She'd never seen him in any other color but white, black, or gray. He looked wonderful in blue, she marveled. And the loose fitting pajamas somehow accentuated the muscular hardness of his body. She swallowed a gulp of her cola, holding the aluminum can with nervous fingers. Her thoughts seemed to be heading compulsively in a dangerous direction.

"I have some spare pajama tops in the bottom drawer," he said. He was watching her, his ebony eyes riveted to her face. "Why don't you have a hot shower and slip into one of them? Then we can go to bed."

She choked on her cola. He took the can from her and leaned forward to stroke her throat. "Are you all right, precious?"

"Justin, don't!" She was already beginning to rethink her promise to spend the night. Justin's headache seemed to have miraculously disappeared, sans pain pills, and he looked vital and virile and overwhelmingly, devastatingly masculine. "I'll sleep in my clothes," she said firmly, backing away from his caressing fingers. "And I'll sleep on the sofa."

"You're liable to get nightmares from that print," he warned with a smile. "And it's too short and too narrow to be comfortable." He caught her hand and carried it to his mouth, pressing his lips against her palm. "Sleep in my bed with me, Stacey."

His evocative words and his loverlike touch sent a curl of desire spiraling through her. She drew back her hand with a half groan. "Justin, this is insane!"

"Don't be afraid of me, Stacey," he said huskily. "Let me hold you tonight. That's all I want—to hold you in my arms all through the night."

She felt herself being drawn into the dark warmth of his ebony eyes. It would be so easy to say yes! she thought. She was suddenly drained, completely exhausted both physically and emotionally. The sleepless night before, the tensions of the day, and the demands of pregnancy on her body combined to hit her with a mind-numbing fatigue.

"The doctor said you must have rest and quiet, Justin," she reminded him. "That precludes—"

"Yes, sweetheart," he interrupted, grinning. "That certainly does preclude . . ."

He was touching her again, stroking her arms from wrist to shoulder, and her brain clouded. "Come to bed, Stacey," he said softly, "and we'll go to sleep."

She nodded sleepily, not allowing herself to think. She walked slowly to the bathroom, too tired to take a shower, too tired to do anything but take off her dress and her too-tight bra and slip into Justin's dark blue pajama top. She washed her face and padded back into the bedroom.

Justin pulled back the covers and welcomed her into the bed. The mattress was firm and comfortable, and Stacey allowed herself the luxury of sinking into the pillows and savoring the soft warmth of the goose-down comforter. Outside, the wind blew the rain against the windowpane. She felt warm and safe and glad to be inside, to be in this bed with Justin. Fatigue seemed to circulate through her veins, drugging her. Stacey closed her eyes.

And opened them a moment later. Justin's fingers had slipped beneath the elastic waistbands of her black tights and panties. "Why don't you take these off, sweetheart?" His voice was soft and silky. "You'll be so much more comfortable without them."

She caught his fingers and carefully removed them. "Justin," she murmured, her voice sleepy and thick, "give me a very, very, very large break."

He laughed, a deep, rich sound, and pulled her against him, into the curve of his body. "Go to sleep, Stacey." His breath rustled her hair as she snuggled, spoon-fashion, against him.

She was almost asleep when she remembered Brynn. For safety reasons, the two had agreed long ago always to keep each other informed as to their whereabouts. "Justin." She wriggled in his arms. "I have to call Brynn and tell her where I am."

He dialed the number for her without question or complaint. There were times when his practicality was quite a worthwhile trait, she decided. He held her in his arms, under the warmth of the covers, as she talked to Brynn.

"I'm glad you're starting to work things out with him, Stace," Brynn said after Stacey explained that she was spending the night.

"Brynnie, it's not what you think—"

"Yes, it is, Brynn," Justin said loudly. "It's exactly what you think."

"Justin!" admonished Stacey, blushing.

Brynn laughed. "You're really loosening the guy up, Stace. He never used to make jokes or sexual innuendos."

"Oh, he's a regular comedian!" Stacey gave Justin a playful punch in the arm and he held her still in an escape-proof trap of his arms and legs. She squirmed and wiggled in his grasp, giggling in spite of herself. Justin gave a throaty stage villain's laugh and held firm. Brynn, on the other end of the line, was momentarily forgotten.

Brynn cleared her throat. "Stace, I hate to inject a sour note into all this fun, but you'll never guess who I found skulking around our building tonight. Cord Marshall! He claimed he was looking for you."

Justin heard her and stiffened. "Marshall?"

"I'm sure he *was* looking for me, Brynn. I'm going to be on his show on Saturday night," Stacey said blithely.

"You're what?" Brynn gasped.

"You're *not*!" Justin growled.

Stacey tried to shake him off, but he wouldn't release her. "I had dinner with Cord the other night, Brynnie. Actually, he was surprisingly nice and I promised to—"

"Nice?" echoed Brynn. "Stacey, the man is pond scum. You'd have been safer having dinner with a typhoid carrier."

Justin took the receiver from Stacey. "Don't worry, Brynn. She isn't going on that show. Nor will there be any more dinners with the 'nice' man."

Stacey scowled and snatched the receiver back. "Brynnie—"

"Stacey, for once Justin Marks and I are in complete agreement. Marshall is a total creep. He tried to pump me for information about your family. Turned on what he thinks is his irresistible charm and even had the nerve to make a pass at me!"

"Cord Marshall made a pass at you?" Stacey squealed. "What did you do, Brynnie?"

"Remember when Lucas gave us those lessons in self-defense?" Brynn asked dryly. "Well, I got to try out my skills for the first time on Cord Marshall. It works, Stace."

"Oh, I wish I could've been there!"

"Bloodthirsty little thing," Justin said with a wry smile. "Tell Brynn to bring you something to wear tomorrow," he added. "She can drop it off on her way to work in the morning."

"Orders received," Brynn said before Stacey could speak. "Something loose-fitting and comfortable, huh, Stace?"

"Good night, Brynn," Stacey said.

Justin took the receiver from her and replaced it in its cradle. His hands sought her breasts. "Now where were we?"

"We were almost asleep," she said sternly, moving his hands to her waist. It didn't occur to her to move away from him. Instead she cuddled close as his big arms enfolded her. "Good night, Justin," she whispered drowsily.

"Good night . . . my darling."

Six

"Stacey, where in the hell are my pants?"
demanded an irate Justin Marks. He'd showered,
shaved, and dressed in a stiffly starched white
shirt, a gray suit coat, dark tie, socks, and white
briefs. His closet door stood open and he surveyed
his wardrobe with an exasperated growl. "There
isn't a single pair of trousers in here!"

"I told you that you weren't going to work today,
Justin." Stacey watched him with an amused grin.
"The doctor prescribed rest and quiet and that's
what you're going to have. Now, get back into bed
and I'll bring you your breakfast."

"Dammit, I don't want any breakfast! I want my
pants! What did you do with them? All eight pairs
are missing."

"They're locked in the trunk of your car," she
said smugly. "And I have the key. I drove them to
the supermarket this morning while you were
sleeping. I knew you'd insist on going to work
today, and I also knew you wouldn't get very far
without any trousers."

"You locked all my pants in the trunk of my car?"
he repeated incredulously.

She nodded. "And then I called Dad's office and
told them that you wouldn't be in. I also called my
mother and told her to tell Dad that you were

injured and weren't to be bothered by a trillion phone calls from the staff."

"You've certainly been busy this morning, haven't you?" Justin scowled. "Stacey, it's almost ten o'clock. I've never slept so late in my life! And I *have* to go to the office!"

"The pain pill knocked you out," she told him. "I gave it to you around five o'clock when I got up to—" Well, she thought, there was no need to elaborate. But she'd taken the anti-nausea medication then and had given Justin a pain pill, in case he was in pain. He'd been barely awake and had obediently swallowed the pill without question.

"You drugged me!" he accused her. "I never take pills of any kind. I never even take an aspirin."

The pill had indeed knocked Justin out, Stacey mused. He'd slept through Brynn's arrival at eight-thirty and Stacey's departure for the supermarket at nine. Taking his pants had been a veritable brainstorm, and she congratulated herself. Otherwise, Justin would have been dressed and gone by the time she returned from the store. "I stocked your kitchen," she said, adjusting the sleeves of her pink-and-gray sweat suit. Brynn had bought the sweat suit when she'd taken up running in a fitness craze that had lasted less than a week. The loose-fitting pants and top were ideal for Stacey in her current condition. Brynn had brought along socks and sneakers too. "And you owe me a hundred and fifty-five dollars for the groceries," Stacey added.

"What?" he yelled.

"You needed everything, Justin, right down to salt and pepper. Now what would you like for breakfast? Oatmeal? Eggs? Bacon?" With the aid of that marvelous medicine, Stacey could face it all. "I even bought tomato juice and frozen Danishes."

"I want my pants, Stacey!"

"You're beginning to sound like a record with the needle stuck in a groove, Justin."

"Where are my car keys?"

"In a place where you won't find them." They were in her bra. She cast him a triumphant grin. "Now put on your pajamas and get into bed like a good boy." He glowered at her. "Maybe you'd like a nice hot-water bottle to take with you?" she asked gleefully.

He advanced toward her, his black eyes glittering. "This has gone on long enough, Stacey." He towered over her, but she met his gaze squarely, refusing to be intimidated. "Just calm down, Justin. You're going to get another headache."

"I never had a headache. I never had any pain at all. I was faking it."

"Last night you were lying on that bed moaning with pain, Justin Marks. I saw you. I *heard* you."

"There wasn't a damn thing wrong with me. I just wanted you to stay so I pretended my head hurt."

"Oh, sure!" she said mockingly. "I understand, Justin. In the light of day, Mr. Macho can't admit to experiencing pain or displaying weakness of any kind. Don't worry, though. Your little secret is safe with me." She reached up to give his cheek a rather patronizing pat.

"Female chauvinist," he growled. "You're enjoying this, aren't you?"

"Don't make it so difficult for yourself, Justin. Just give in and let me take care of you." Her own words temporarily disconcerted her. She wanted to take care of him with a fierceness that would not be denied. Quickly, she turned away and headed toward the kitchen. She concentrated on the task of making his breakfast: scrambled eggs, bacon, a glass of tomato juice, and a blueberry Danish.

She was transferring everything to a plate when

she became aware of Justin standing in the doorway, watching her. He was wearing a fresh pair of blue pajamas and she smiled at him, amused at his grudging acquiescence. Their eyes met, and for an electrifying moment Stacey felt some intangible but compelling force pass between them and hold firm. It was impossible to tear her gaze from his.

"I like having you here, in my apartment," he said huskily. "In my kitchen, in my bed."

She drew in her breath sharply. The occasion called for a light, witty comeback to lessen the tension-filled awareness between them, but her mind seemed to have gone blank. He came to stand behind her and his arms encircled her waist, drawing her back against the length of his hard, strong body. His lips nuzzled her neck and her knees went weak. She leaned into him, her eyelids closing heavily.

His hands moved upward to cup her breasts, his thumbs flicking over the nipples, which were already becoming taut. "Are they sore today?" he whispered against her ear, and his tongue played with the soft lobe. "Does it hurt if I touch your breasts, love?"

"N-No," she breathed, and the plate slipped from her fingers and clattered into the sink. "Your breakfast," she murmured breathlessly as Justin swung her up into his arms.

"I'm not hungry for food." He carried her from the kitchen into the bedroom, his stride brisk and determined. "Only for you, darling." He laid her down on the bed and sat on the edge of it, carefully untying the shoelaces of her sneakers.

"Justin, your head . . . This . . . We . . ."

"You're taking excellent care of me, Stacey," he assured her, tossing her shoes and socks to the floor. "You sent me to bed and now you're going to take a nap with me."

He undressed her with dizzying speed, and when he found the key in her bra, he merely smiled and laid it on the nightstand. She wanted him, she admitted to herself as she lay beneath his caressing hands. His dark eyes were watching her, studying every line and curve of her body, and a hot, honeyed response flowed through her.

She trembled as his fingers moved purposefully over the taut peaks of her breasts. "So hard and tight," he said, his voice deep and intimate. "Do you remember that night in August when you asked me to kiss you there?"

She expelled a tensely held breath. "Justin . . ."

"Do you want me to kiss your nipples now, Stacey?" he said against the creamy smooth skin of her neck. He smiled hotly when she moaned and arched up to him. "I want to kiss you everywhere. Here . . . and here . . ." His mouth brushed her nipples, then moved to her navel, and then below. "I want to taste every inch of you, my sweet, my baby."

She felt as if she were on fire. A wild little cry escaped from her throat and she tried to stifle it by covering her mouth with her fist.

"No, love." He removed her hand and kissed her knuckles, her wrist, her palm. "I want to hear you. I want to hear just what I'm making you feel."

"Oh, Justin!" She wrapped her arms around his neck and pulled him down to her, desperate, starving for his mouth on hers. She felt his body against hers, hot and hungry and hard, and she moved sinuously against him in a way that inflamed them both. She felt delirious with wanting him, with needing him.

"Love me, Justin," she cried out when the exquisite pleasure of his hands and his lips had her burning with a hot, helpless urgency. She knew a fierce need to possess him—and to be totally possessed by him.

"Yes, baby," he whispered, his eyes glowing with passion. He entered her softness and she welcomed him with a passionate, enveloping shudder.

I love you, she cried silently, wrapping herself around him and clinging to him as he moved within her. Her feelings for him transcended the mere physical pleasure he gave her. This was not just sex. They were making love in the fullest sense. She loved him and she was carrying his child. It was elemental, natural, and right. They belonged together.

"Don't hold back, Stacey," he said hoarsely. "Come with me, love. Now . . . now!"

She gave herself completely to him and cried his name as they both tumbled over the edge into a warm, sensuous sea of rapture.

It was a long time before either of them surfaced. Tingling in the warmth of a sensual afterglow, Stacey stretched beneath him and sighed with contentment.

Justin lifted his head and gazed into her eyes, which were soft and golden with love. "I love you," he said, his night-dark eyes holding hers.

A wild spasm of joy ricocheted through her.

"I've loved you for years, Stacey. I wanted to tell you in August, but you . . ." He smiled suddenly and lightly kissed the tip of her nose. "You went screaming into the bathroom and locked me out."

She threaded her hands through his thick hair. "I—I'm sorry, Justin. I was so—so . . ."

"Used to hating me. I know, sweet."

"You hated me, too, Justin," she reminded him shakily.

"No." He shook his head. "That isn't true at all." He gazed into space, a faraway look in his eyes. "The first time I saw you I thought you were the cutest, brightest, liveliest little girl I'd ever met. You were just fifteen years old and vivacious and bubbling with animation and energy. I was fascinated with you. I couldn't ever seem to take my eyes off you."

"Justin." She squirmed beneath him. "You're romanticizing. You thought I was a brat."

"You *are* a brat," he agreed with a chuckle, and she kicked him in the ankle with her bare foot. "But that didn't stop me from loving you, Stacey. It hit me the summer you turned sixteen. I'd come down to Rehoboth Beach for a meeting with your father—"

"I remember. It was the first time I'd ever seen anyone on the beach in a gray suit and black wing-tip shoes. A violation you manage to repeat every summer."

He laughed, and the happiness in his face sent a surge of pleasure through her veins. She couldn't ever remember seeing Justin look so relaxed and carefree and just plain happy.

"You were in a pink bathing suit," he recalled with a smile, which faded somewhat when he added, "and you were with some brainless, blond high-school boy."

"Mmm, I remember him. Derek Rivers. You're right, he *was* brainless. But he had a lot of brawn, which impressed me back then."

"When I saw the two of you cavorting together on the beach, when I saw the stupid little twerp put his arm around you . . ." Justin paused and his face darkened. "I felt as if a knife had been plunged into my gut. I realized then that I wasn't merely amused by a captivating little teenager. I felt possessive toward you—I thought of you as *mine*! I wanted to drown that young punk and carry you away, to keep you with me forever."

"Oh, Justin," Stacey breathed. He was looking

into her eyes so deeply. She felt an odd tremor of trepidation as the intensity of his emotions enveloped her.

"I couldn't have you, of course," he continued softly. "You were only sixteen years old—and the daughter of the man whose goals and aspirations were so linked with mine. A thirty-year-old AA does *not* fall in love with the senator's teenage daughter. I had to fight it, Stacey. I made myself be as abrupt and as harsh toward you as I could possibly be. I wanted to—I *needed* to—incite your hostility. I needed that distance between us or I would have . . . I couldn't have stopped myself from . . ." His voice trailed off. "I had to make you dislike me intensely," he finished flatly.

"You certainly did a masterful job of it." She frowned thoughtfully. It was all so strange, so totally incredible. To think that all these years when she'd thought he hated her, he'd really wanted her. She felt as if she'd stepped through the looking glass into a world where "nothing is as it seems." She stared at him, bewildered.

"I did *too* masterful a job," he said ruefully. "When you were finally older, when I brought you to Capitol Hill to work, I thought I could break down the barriers between us. . . ." He paused and gave his head a slight shake. "But you were so hostile toward me, so accustomed to hating me. I couldn't get past those walls you'd built against me. I would've despaired completely if you hadn't always been so aware of me, so quick to antagonize me and provoke me. You'd behaved that way toward me since you were in your teens and I thought, I hoped, it meant that you were fighting your attraction to me too."

"Grace said I was always teasing you," Stacey murmured, her eyes wide with wonder. "My Lord, all these years . . . Justin, it's too unbelievable to be true! I *know* we were really enemies!"

"Who were fighting against becoming lovers. Think of that night last August, Stacey. That was no drunken one-night stand. It was the result of years of sexual tension and suppressed attraction."

"No!" She felt obliged to protest.

"Yes." His mouth opened over hers and she responded instantly and passionately, without thought of resistance. It was her helpless, mindless response to him that convinced her. Her body had known she wanted Justin Marks long before her mind had acknowledged the fact.

He kissed her deeply, possessively, and she luxuriated in the feel of his heavy, hair-roughened body over hers. "I want you again," he whispered softly. "Are you ready for me, my love?"

"Oh, yes, Justin," she heard herself say in a throaty, sexy voice she hardly recognized as her own. She opened herself to him completely, lovingly. She was already so aroused and ready for him that she welcomed the stunning power of his possession with a breathless cry of need. Passion flared to a white-hot clumination and she was once again swept away and melted by the glow.

"I love to watch you," he said later, when their passion had cooled. He was lying beside her, propped on his elbow as he gently stroked her hair. "The way your lips are parted and wet, the way you close your eyes so tightly, the sexy little sounds you make."

Stacey blushed. Despite the intimacies they had shared, his observation was more than a little unnerving. To have exposed herself to him so completely made her feel frighteningly vulnerable.

"Do you think you'd like a White House wedding?" he asked, his jet-black eyes alight with humor. "Spence and Patty's little girls could be the flower girls—they can wear their pink dresses, *not* their overalls—and Lucas can be my best man. Can you visualize him slipping me the ring in a tricky underhanded pass rush?"

"White House wedding?" she repeated, her mouth suddenly dry. "That's not funny, Justin."

"We could be married before, of course, darling." He took her in his arms. "But I thought you and your mother might be too busy with the campaign to plan the kind of wedding you'll want. Since you are your parents' only daughter, I'm sure they want to have a big, splashy wedding, and that's fine with me."

Perhaps the only thing Stacey loathed more than campaigning was the thought of herself as the bride in a mammoth wedding extravaganza. She and Brynn had decided at age thirteen that eloping made much more sense, and neither had seen fit to change their minds since. And here was Justin, talking about a White House wedding, a mammoth wedding extravaganza right up there on a level with royal weddings, the most mammoth extravaganza of them all.

Her heart began to thud against her ribs. The closeness, the intimacy, and the ecstasy evaporated, to be replaced by a cold, sickly feeling of dread. It should be so simple. She loved Justin and he loved her and she was carrying their child. But the world didn't consist of just the three of them. Justin's reference to the campaign—to the White House!—underscored that.

She struggled out of his arms and sat up in bed, holding the sheet against her with trembling fingers. "Justin, we—I—I can't marry you."

His big hand closed over hers and he deliberately, carefully lowered the sheet. "Oh, yes, Stacey. You can and you will."

She was naked and vulnerable and suddenly very

afraid. Marry Justin? she thought. Live in Washington in the relentless glare of politics, endure a marriage with a husband physically absent ninety percent of the time and mentally preoccupied the remaining ten percent, when he was home? Spend a lifetime explaining their father's absences to their children, watching them hurt from his never-ending neglect as he dedicated his time and talent to others, but never his family? Suffering through the endless cycle of campaign after campaign, spending night after night, weekend after weekend, alone? Or worse, joining him on the campaign trail, which she had always found exhausting and dehumanizing?

All her life she had promised herself that her marriage would be different from the life she had known. She wanted a family-oriented man with a consuming interest in his wife and children. Justin Marks, a political wunderkind with his goals and ambition centered on the White House with her father, was totally opposite from the mythical man of her dreams. And though she loved him, though their child was growing within her, she could not marry him. She just couldn't!

"What is it, Stacey?" Justin sat up and cupped her chin in his hand, turning her head toward him. "I know you love me, too, although you haven't said the words." His voice lowered, his tone growing fierce. "You wouldn't have surrendered so absolutely if you didn't. You gave yourself to me completely and I intend to keep what belongs to me."

"It would be very convenient for you, wouldn't it, Justin?" She sighed wearily. "Being Bradford Lipton's son-in-law."

"Dammit, Stacey, don't accuse me of that! I love you. The fact that Bradford Lipton is your father has nothing to do with us."

"You're wrong, Justin, it has everything to do with us. I grew up as a child in a political marriage and the last thing I want to be is a wife in one. I'm not like my mother, Justin. Sometimes I wish I were, but I'm not and I can never be. She's subordinated herself and her marriage to her husband's political career, but I want my husband to be intensely involved with me and our life. I want the father of my children to be with me while I'm in labor, not somewhere off giving a speech in another state! And I want my kids to have a full-time father. I want him to be home in the evenings to help them with their homework and I want him to be available for all their dopey school programs. I missed all of that as a child and I won't allow my children to miss it too."

Justin said nothing. What could he say? she asked herself. She reached for the sheet to cover her naked body and he did not stop her. They both knew that in his current position, and in his future one, working for her father, he could never meet the demands she was making. There was a long, dejected silence.

"This is the most ridiculous argument we've ever had," Justin said at last, scowling his impatience. "We're talking about hypothetical children in a hypothetical marriage. Let's confine ourselves to the present, Stacey. To you and me and the way we feel about each other right now."

Could she have done it if she weren't pregnant? Stacey wondered. Would she have allowed herself to don a pair of rose-colored glasses and consider only the passion-filled present? But the undeniable existence of their very *unhypothetical* child forced her to look into the future. And what she saw there thoroughly depressed her. And frightened her too.

"Do you know how much I hate living in politics,

Justin?" she asked softly. "I guess I'll have to tell you. I despise it, I loathe it, it's poison to me. I hated it as a child and as a teenager and I hate it now. I hate the limelight. I hate the campaigns and the crowds and the hand-shaking and all the noise. It's a lonely life, even though there are always too many people around. There are no real friends, only temporary allies. People smile, but they're wearing masks, and you never get to see behind them. I'll never, never marry anyone connected with politics, Justin. I'd rather spend my life alone than do that."

They stared at each other for several long moments, and then Justin spoke, his voice flat. "I had no idea you were so strongly opposed to the political life, Stacey. Oh, you've always railed about the inconveniences and the problems, but I didn't realize your feelings ran so deep. I thought you were—uh—just being difficult."

"I think I probably *am* difficult, Justin." Her lips twisted into a sad smile. "I know enough about myself to realize that I'm rather demanding and that I need attention. I can be loving and happy with it and miserable and bitchy without it. I'm an extremely poor candidate for a political wife."

It was all so hopeless, she thought. She felt as if she were lost in a bizarre labyrinth with no way out. She felt like crying; she couldn't help herself. Good grief, she *was* crying! There were tears streaming down her cheeks and she choked back a sudden sob.

"Sweetheart, don't cry." Justin took her in his arms and cradled her against his chest, but Stacey cried harder. It was so much worse, being in love with him. If only she could go back to the days when she thought she hated *him* as well as politics. But now . . .

"Please don't cry, Stacey." He rocked her gently,

his voice coaxing. "Let's make it easier, sweet. We'll take one step at a time. We won't discuss marriage at all. I promise not to bring the subject up again. Let's just enjoy what we have now."

"Just have an affair, you mean?" she asked in a strangled voice.

"Yes, darling, we'll just have an affair," he said soothingly.

Was that supposed to be comforting? she wondered, stiffening. The man she loved, whose child she carried, had just told her to forget about marriage, that he was perfectly willing to settle for an affair instead. She stopped crying. He'd certainly made his decision easily enough. He had listened to what she wanted in a husband and quickly opted out. Politics was his life, and a steamy little affair with her on the side was quite enough for him.

She scowled and wrenched herself out of his arms. She climbed out of bed and began to gather up her clothes, which were scattered over the floor.

"Stacey, there is one more thing we have to discuss." Justin stood up, splendidly naked and completely comfortable with his nudity. Her gaze flicked over his powerful, virile body, and her own body heated with a primitive, feminine response.

"Darling, when I'm with you, I completely lose my head," Justin admitted in a sheepish tone that tugged at her heart. Virtually everything about the man appealed to her today, she reluctantly acknowledged to herself. She was absurdly, undeniably in love with him.

He cleared his throat. "I seem to forget—I never even think of—" He stared at her as she gracefully stepped into her silky white panties and made a sound halfway between a sigh and a groan. "Stacey, when I made love to you this morning, I didn't take any precautions. Not either time."

Stacey's heart gave a crazy lurch and the lacy white bra she held in her hands dropped to the bed. His voice buzzed around her head as he continued. "And I wanted to ask . . . Stacey, are you, that is, do you—"

"Are you trying to ask if I'm on the pill?" she interrupted him. She couldn't stand to listen to him skirt the issue for another second. It must be the first time in living memory that Justin Marks wasn't boldly setting forth his assertion. "Fine time to ask, Justin. Rather like closing the barn door *after* the horse has escaped."

She had the satisfaction of seeing his cheeks begin to redden. He hadn't managed to think of precautions last August either, she thought. Neither of them had. Stacey gulped. She wasn't about to remind him of that! It would be dangerous for him to connect that night with a lack of precaution. She forced a saucy smile. "I do appreciate your concern, though, Justin." She tried hard to sound flippant, hoping to divert him from thinking back to when they'd first made love.

Justin was most disconcerted. "Sweetheart, I know it was irresponsible, selfish, and totally thoughtless of me," he said with real remorse. "Not to mention incredibly callow." She felt his jet-black eyes upon her as she fumbled again with her bra. Moving lithely, he caught her in his arms and pulled her back against him.

"You have a mind-shattering effect on me, love," he murmured huskily, caressing the sensitive softness of her neck with his lips. "Taking you in my arms is like taking the most potent of drugs." His hands smoothed over the soft thickness of her waist and the rounding curve of her hip, then slowly explored her belly's slight swelling before claiming her full breasts.

"Stacey, if there are any . . . results . . . of this

morning . . ." His voice was thoughtful and Stacey felt a rising apprehension. Was he remembering the first time he had explored her body, nearly three months ago? Was he contrasting the then-supple curves with this new, burgeoning ripeness? She sucked in her breath.

"There won't be any results," she said firmly. Not this time, at least, she amended silently. The results had already occurred. "It's—uh—safe, Justin."

"But you're not on the pill," he said with unnerving conviction.

"Will you just drop it?" she exclaimed sharply. Fat chance of that, she thought, groaning silently. Justin could be as tenacious as a migraine headache. Nevertheless, she tried to divert him. "The timing isn't right for my getting pregnant, remember? Now, go eat your breakfast. It's in the kitchen, undoubtedly stone cold by now."

"But you want me to eat it anyway." His eyes gleamed with sudden humor.

"Yes."

"Sounds tempting at that." He grinned at her. "I've often had a yearning for cold, congealing eggs."

He was actually going to drop the subject of the pill and precautionless lovemaking! she thought with amazement, breathing a silent sigh of relief. She watched him pull on his underwear, then reach for his white shirt.

"Stacey," he said suddenly, his dark eyes fixed on her. "You know that I'd marry you if—"

"I know, Justin," she interrupted quickly. Of course, he hadn't given up. He'd merely used a diversionary tactic himself to offset her. Suppose he decided to watch her closely for possible "results of this morning"? Stacey was shaking as she pulled on Brynn's pink-and-gray jogging suit.

What he would eventually see were the results of their August passion.

And suppose he insisted on marrying her? Could she be forced into a marriage she didn't want? On the other hand, could she face a pregnancy alone and unmarried? She tried to visualize herself huge and swollen in the ninth month of pregnancy and simply couldn't. She was still practicing some denial, she realized gloomily. She was still keeping the full reality of the situation somewhat at bay.

Out of the corner of her eye, she saw Justin reach for the key to his car, and she flew to the nightstand to retrieve it.

"I thought I'd demonstrated that I was perfectly fit," he said archly as he watched her palm the key.

"The doctor said you weren't to plunge into that fatiguing, frenetic schedule of yours," she retorted. "And we're going to follow the doctor's orders."

"Oh, are *we*?" He seemed suddenly amused. He looked incredibly vital and vibrant, attractively male. Stacey's breath caught in her throat.

"Are you going to stay with me every minute to make sure I follow doctor's orders?" He flashed a challenging, sexy grin.

She was so in love with him, she thought. And what were a few more days of suspending reality? She moved close and wrapped her arms around his waist. "I'm not going to let you out of my sight," she said huskily.

He slowly lowered her down on the bed. "What a shame we bothered to dress. Now we have to take the time to take all these clothes off again."

She kissed him lovingly, then sat back up. "We're not staying here all day, Justin." He had ably demonstrated that he wasn't suffering any ill effects from his concussion, and a day spent alone with him in his apartment translated into a day spent in bed with him. And though part of her wanted it, craved it, the sensible, practical part of her vetoed the idea as resolutely dangerous.

"No?" He slipped his hand under her sweat shirt and stroked her bare back with his fingertips. "What are we going to do today, Stacey?"

"We're going shopping," she announced, and laughed at his expression of total astonishment.

Seven

"Shopping?" Justin stared at her as though she'd taken permanent leave of her senses. "For what?"

"For clothes. For you. We'll go to a nice suburban mall and buy you some clothes that aren't gray suits, white shirts, and navy ties."

She expected him to argue, or even to flatly refuse. To her own astonishment he agreed without a word of protest. She drove him to Montgomery County's sumptuous White Flint Mall and dragged him into Bloomingdale's to begin his transformation. He agreed to a teal-blue, V-neck sweater and immediately decided to wear it over his tie-less, coat-less white shirt. He also agreed to a pair of tan cords, a tan sweater, and a yellow shirt, but positively balked at blue jeans. "They remind me of Spence and Patty's farm," he said, his jaw set in a familiar, stubborn line. "And I refuse to wear overalls, either, Stacey."

"I wasn't about to ask you to," she replied haughtily, then spoiled the effect by giggling at the mental vision of Justin Marks in overalls, carrying a pitchfork.

She selected a cotton rugby shirt with bright green, red, and white stripes, ignoring his plaintive, "I'll look like the Italian flag." She also insisted that he buy a comfortable pair of cordovan loafers.

"This is just the beginning, Justin," she said expansively as they carried the purchases to the car. "There's a whole world of color out there. Pink shirts, kelly-green blazers, plaid slacks—"

Justin feigned horror. "Not worn together, I hope?"

She ignored him. "Shorts, sport shirts, bathing suits," she continued to rhapsodize. "No more looking like an FBI agent making an arrest when you come down to the beach."

"Stacey, the only times I've been to your family's beach house have been for business meetings with the senator. It would have been inappropriate for me to show up dressed to swim. Presumptuous too. It wasn't as if I were an invited guest."

Was that a trace of wistfulness in his tone? she wondered. She glanced at him covertly, her tawny eyes darkening with emotion. Justin had never been invited socially to their beach house? His only appearances there were official business meetings with the vacationing senator? She felt a pang of shame. Her parents—and she herself!—had been terribly remiss. All these years Justin had driven the two and a half hours to Rehoboth Beach in Delaware and then driven back to the city without taking a dip in the surf because he hadn't been invited to. Yet he considered himself close to the Liptons, thought of them as his vicarious family.

A wave of sadness rolled over her. "Oh, Justin," she said softly. Before she had even realized what she was doing, she slipped her hand into the crook of his elbow. He pressed it firmly against the side of his body in a possessive gesture of silent acknowledgment.

"Let me take you to dinner tonight." Justin was stroking Stacey's hair as she lay in his arms.

They'd returned to his apartment after their shopping trip and gone directly to bed. "Do you realize it will be our first real date?"

"You do have an original approach, Justin." She smiled languidly at him. "Asking me for a date, our first date, while we're in bed together." She stretched languorously and snuggled against him. It was pure heaven to be held like this, to have Justin tenderly stroke her hair as he caressed her with his eyes. That Justin Marks had a deeply romantic streak was probably the best-kept secret in the Western world, she mused. But he had. He laced his fingers with hers when they held hands, he gazed deeply into her eyes while she spoke, and he listened to every word she said. And when they made love, he was just as attentive afterward as before.

"We'll stop by your apartment so you can change clothes," he said. "And then—" He paused and Stacey felt him tense. "Stacey, you'll stay here tonight." It was a command, yet she heard the unspoken plea in his words.

She was too in love to refuse. She wanted him relaxed and happy, wanted to see his dark eyes glowing with contentment. Once again she decided to put the future on hold and live for the moment. She and Justin were alone in their own private world, and for now she would let that be enough. "Yes, Justin." She reached up to kiss him. "I'll stay tonight."

They had dinner in a dark, quiet little restaurant in Georgetown, where they sat at a corner table and talked softly over the flickering candlelight. What surprised Stacey was how easily the conversation flowed between them. By tacit agreement, politics was not mentioned, and a thoroughly political animal like Justin Marks should have sunk hopelessly into silence. He was not good at small talk, didn't go to the latest movies or read the current best-sellers, didn't watch television or read *People* magazine. All of which were the mainstay of Stacey's usual date conversation.

But she was insatiably curious about Justin the man and she found herself asking him personal questions, drawing him out, until somehow they were both freely discussing ideas and past experiences and opinions. The conversation never once flagged. Talking with Justin was exhilarating and absorbing for Stacey. She couldn't ever remember having such a wonderful time on a dinner date.

They lingered over coffee and dessert for a long time, until the waiter began to hover surreptitiously and Justin glanced at his watch. "It's eleven-thirty!" he said with surprise.

Stacey glanced quickly around the restaurant. They were the only ones left, with the exception of the waiters. Evenings tended to end early during the week in Washington, but she wasn't ready to end this one. "Let's go somewhere to dance," she suggested, half-expecting Justin to refuse.

He didn't. "I do want to warn you that I'm an atrocious dancer," he said. "I managed to learn some sort of box step, but I doubt that many would call it dancing."

"You mainly shuffle political dowagers around the floor for duty dances," she guessed.

He nodded and laughed. "My lack of a social life precluded any need for dancing lessons. I only dance when it's absolutely unavoidable and my partners tend to be on the wrong side of sixty."

"What about the boiler-room girls?" she asked, thinking of the many attractive young women who signed on to help in her father's various campaigns. Justin was the one closest to the candidate himself and she knew that the aura of his power would be incredibly attractive to some. "They're always throwing parties, aren't they?" Her brother Sterne was forever crashing them, hoping to score. "Hasn't one of the boiler-room girls offered to teach you to dance?" she demanded, suddenly, fiercely jealous at the thought.

Justin smiled. "I'm too unapproachable, you know that, Stacey. Who wants to teach a tyrannical, humorless, methodical robot to dance?"

She stared at him. Yes, she'd called him all those things—and worse. Her face flushed. Underneath his cold political veneer, he wasn't any of those things. She knew that now. And she was the only person in Washington, anywhere, who knew the warmly romantic, passionate, and thoughtful man within. She smiled at him, her eyes glowing.

They ended up in a quiet little club in Southwest Washington, where the band alternated fast and slow songs, old standards and current favorites. On the small dance floor, Stacey clasped her arms around Justin's neck and pressed herself close to him.

"I bet this isn't the way you dance with old Mrs. Weatherby at an Omaha fund-raiser," she teased, laying her head against his chest and closing her eyes.

His arms encircled her and he gave up his self-taught box step simply to sway slightly to the music. "I never knew dancing could be so enjoyable," he murmured, and Stacey smiled at the thickness of his voice. His thighs were hard against her and she slowly, sexily undulated her hips against his. The impulse to rub her breasts against his chest was irresistible and she gave into it without further thought.

"Stacey!" He groaned as his big hands moved heavily over her back. "You're not wearing a bra," he said huskily, and she shook her head. She was wearing a full-cut, black-velvet jumper—a Brynn impulse-and-never-worn purchase from several seasons back—along with a white silk blouse. A bra hadn't been necessary, and she'd gratefully skipped the restricting garment. Her bras were uncomfortably tight these days, as were all her clothes. She really had to buy some things that fit, Stacey thought lazily as she clung to Justin. Brynn's closet was bound to run out of old rejects she could borrow.

Stacey stiffened abruptly. Good Lord, for a while she'd actually managed to forget, but the mundane wardrobe problem brought her firmly back to earth. She was pregnant, and only she and Brynn knew it! This little idyll with Justin was merely a very brief respite from the terrible storm that was about to hit. She seemed to be getting bigger by the day. Her secret baby wasn't going to stay secret much longer.

"What's the matter, love?" Justin whispered, and it both unnerved and touched her that he was so attuned to her every nuance, that he knew something was wrong although she hadn't said a word.

"I'm—I'm tired," she said, because she had to say something. If she were to deny anything was the matter, Justin would continue to probe until . . . He was so thorough, so dogged in his pursuits. . . . Oh, Lord, what was she going to do when he found out?

"Then let's leave, sweetheart." He led her from the dance floor, keeping her close to him, his arm firmly around her. "As much as I enjoy dancing with you, there are other things I enjoy doing with you even more."

She was quiet during the drive back to his apartment, but she sat close to him in the car, her hand on his thigh and her head on his shoulder, her eyes closed. Justin apparently attributed her silence to sleepiness, for he carried her from the car to his bed and undressed her with swift, deft hands. Stacey enjoyed every minute of the cossetting. She felt cherished and safe and loved. A few minutes later Justin was in bed with her, tucking her spoon-fashion into the curve of his body.

"Good night, honey," he murmured, his lips against her hair.

Her eyes snapped open. "Aren't we going to make love, Justin? You said there were other things you enjoyed more than dancing. . . ."

"There are." She heard the smile in his voice. "One of them is holding you in my arms as you sleep." He kissed the top of her head and tightened his hold on her. "I know how tired you are, Stacey. You could hardly keep your eyes open in the car. Go to sleep, love."

She expected to lie awake the whole night, worrying. But after a few minutes of lying in the dark in Justin's arms and listening to the quiet sound of his steady breathing, her eyelids began to droop. They closed heavily. She was where she wanted to be, warm and at peace with the man she loved.

"Am I allowed to go into the office today?" Justin drawled the next morning as they sat in the small kitchen, eating breakfast.

"No!" Stacey said sternly. She was wearing his blue pajama top and methodically sectioning a grapefruit with a knife. "You need another day of rest before you face that—that zoo on the Hill again." And she wanted another day with him, she confessed silently. She wished she could keep him from ever going back there.

"The zoo!" Justin snapped his fingers. "Now there's an idea. Since the sun is shining for what seems to be the first time in weeks, let's take advantage of it, Stacey. Let's go to the National Zoo. I think I'm the only person in the D.C. area who hasn't seen the pandas."

"You haven't seen the pandas?" She pretended to be shocked. "After years of reading about the intimate details of their life together—on the front pages of the *Post*, no less—you *still* haven't seen them?"

"Remiss of me, I know. Shall we rectify the situation?"

She plunked herself down on his lap and pretended to adjust the lapels of his white toweling robe. "Can we rectify it a little later?" She nibbled delicately on the hard, tanned column of his neck.

When Justin rose to his feet, swinging her high against his chest, she shivered with delicious anticipation. "Insatiable little wench." He smiled down at her with loving amusement as he carried her into the bedroom.

"It's all your fault, you know," she accused tenderly, slipping the robe from his shoulders. "You've gotten me addicted to you."

He kissed her, long and lingeringly. "I love you, Stacey."

Her heart somersaulted in her chest. "And I love you, Justin." If only love were enough. The bleak thought slipped past the protective walls in her mind. But it wasn't, not for them, and sometime soon she was going to have to deal with it. But not now. Stacey gave herself completely to their lovemaking, which was as sublime as ever, and succeeded in keeping all thoughts of the future firmly at bay.

* * *

It was a sunny, crisp November day and Justin and Stacey shared the National Zoo with the inevitable tourists and several busloads of schoolchildren. Justin wore his new loafers, his tan cords, yellow shirt, and tan sweater. He looked wonderful and Stacey couldn't keep her eyes from him. She had located the laundry room in Justin's building and was thus wearing Brynn's red-and-black ensemble again.

They stood at a railing overlooking the pandas' outdoor living area and were soon laughing at the animals' complete lack of antics. One panda snoozed in the sun and didn't move a muscle. Far away from its mate, the other one sat on a rock, equally still. When the panda on the rock turned its head slightly after twenty-five motionless minutes, Justin applauded. "Now *that* was worth waiting for!"

Stacey grinned. "It's another hour and a half till their feeding time. Do you feel like staying to watch?"

"I'm sure that the sight of Hsing-Hsing munching on a carrot is one of life's great moments, but would you mind if we missed it?"

She shook her head, laughing. Justin took her hand, lacing his fingers with hers, and they walked to the nearby souvenir stand, which was filled with panda memorabilia.

"I think we should buy a memento of this visit, Stacey. What would you like? A panda shirt? A panda watch? Panda salt and pepper shakers?"

She eyed the merchandise. "How about none of the above?"

"Oh, I see. You want something a little more practical." And before she could stop him, he bought her a three-foot-high stuffed panda with a bright blue ribbon around its neck.

"You're crazy!" she cried as he dumped the over-sized animal into her arms.

"I'm crazy about you," he corrected her and kissed her right in front of the panda souvenir stand as a giggling group of elementary school-children trooped past them.

They spent the rest of the afternoon back in Justin's apartment, in bed, making love, talking lazily, and making love again. When the phone rang at six-thirty, they were both asleep, having earlier drifted into a deep and sated slumber.

Justin answered the phone. "Marks here." His voice was drowsily husky, nothing at all like his usual sharp stacatto bark, Stacey noted with a sleepy smile of amusement. He handed her the receiver. "It's Brynn."

"Hi, Brynnie." Stacey snuggled against Justin, running her hand along the hard angles of his body with possessive satisfaction.

"Just checking in from the Planet Earth, Stace." Brynn's voice was dry. "I know you two lovers are lost in some galaxy of your own, but there are a few practical details here in the real world we've got to iron out."

Stacey's lips quirked. "Such as?"

"Such as what to tell the people who keep calling you here at our apartment. Your mother has called four times, various friends have called and —worst of all—that odious insect Cord Marshall called. I've been telling them that you're out shopping, but I don't think your mother believed me the last time, Stace."

Stacey's hand stilled and she came abruptly, unpleasantly awake from her blissful dream world. The idyll was over. "I'll be back tonight, Brynn," she said in a tight little voice.

"No!" Justin protested. He lifted her hand to his mouth and pressed his lips against her palm. "Stay with me tonight, Stacey."

"I—I—I'll cook dinner here and then come back," Stacey stammered into the phone. Her gaze locked with Justin's and she felt the forceful pull of his magnetism. His eyes were glittering like brilliant obsidian jewels. There had always been a tautness about Justin Marks, something akin to a coiled spring on the verge of being sprung. Before, he had always directed that tense energy into his work. But for the past two days, she had been the focus of his attentive intensity, and Stacey didn't want to give it up. She felt so close to him now, closer than she'd ever felt to anyone, even Brynn, for there was an intimacy between her and Justin that went beyond what friendship could provide. It went beyond sex too. It was a merging of self, a loss of autonomy that might have been frightening, yet wasn't. She felt complemented and strengthened by Justin, but her own identity remained firmly intact. Perhaps too much intact, she thought bleakly. It would be infinitely easier if she could submerge herself in him, lose herself in the delusion that all she needed in life was him. But it wasn't, and she knew it. Justin in the world of politics was the antithesis of all she'd ever wanted. They would inevitably make each other miserable.

"Stacey, don't go," he said urgently, easing her back on the pillows. "Stay tonight, darling."

Stacey swallowed. She would have to give him up soon enough, for politics was about to reclaim him once again. But she could have one more night with him. Just one more night, her heart pleaded.

"Brynn," she said into the phone, "if I stayed here tonight, I could call my mother back." Justin touched her breast and Stacey inhaled sharply as pleasure flowed through her. "If you wouldn't mind telling anyone else who calls that I'm still—uh—shopping." Justin was kissing her neck and she was melting. A small sigh escaped from her lips.

Brynn chuckled. "I'll tell them you've found the sale of the century, Stace."

"Thanks, Brynn. I'll see you tomorrow." Stacey replaced the receiver and wrapped herself around Justin with a hungry little moan.

Stacey arrived at her father's office at noon the next day, stuffed into Brynn's jeans and an over-sized, banana-yellow knit sweater. Diana Drew, the receptionist, glanced at her disapprovingly, but made no comment on the lateness of the hour or Stacey's attire. Stacey gave her a little wave and proceeded directly to Justin's office.

He was sitting at his desk, dressed in his perpet-ual gray, white, and blue, surrounded by stacks of paper that he was diligently sorting through. Stacey's heart gave a queer little leap at the sight of him. They'd been apart nearly five hours. She'd last seen him when he'd kissed her good-bye that morning as she lay in his bed. He'd been Justin, her lover, then. Now he was Justin Marks, the administrative aide and campaign manager. How would the dichotomy affect their relationship? she wondered as she closed the door behind her and crossed the office to climb into his lap.

"Diana Drew glanced pointedly at her watch as I came in," she said as she settled herself in his arms. She was nervous, she admitted to herself. "I almost told her that the boss gave me special per-mission to come in at noon—while we were in bed this morning."

Justin laughed and kissed her cheek. "Yes, I did, didn't I?" He flipped over a paper, scanned it, then threw it away. "Stacey, honey, I called Cord

Marshall this morning and canceled your alleged appearance on his television show tomorrow."

"Oh, well, I suppose it doesn't matter." She shrugged. It occurred to her that her usual reaction to such a Justin edict would have been to protest forcefully his actions. He hadn't discussed canceling her appearance with her. He hadn't even asked her not to appear. He'd simply canceled the whole thing and told her after the fact. But she hadn't wanted to do the show, anyway, and the matter seemed trivial, certainly not worth quarreling about. "Brynn thinks that Cord Marshall is some creepy species that's cultivated in a petri dish," she added with a grin.

"I happen to agree with her." Justin cupped her chin in his hand and tilted her face upward to kiss her mouth lightly. "I'm glad you realize that your appearance on that show was out of the question, sweet. Thank you for not throwing a tantrum over it."

"I don't throw tantrums," she told him loftily as she teased his lips with her tongue. "I may—um—express my displeasure from time to time, but I don't have tantrums."

"Thank you for clarifying that for me." He smiled. One big hand moved over the curve of her hip, then stopped to rest on her thigh. "Stacey? Sweetheart?"

She lay against him, blissfully content. Maybe Justin wasn't going to be so different in the office, after all, she thought. Maybe . . . "Yes, love?" she asked, her voice tender.

"About these jeans."

She sat up a little. "What about them?"

"You went back to your apartment this morning to change into something appropriate to wear to the office, remember, darling? Well, you must be aware that this . . . costume is as inappropriate for

Senator Lipton's office as the sweat suit or that black-and-red disco dress are."

She clamped her lips over her teeth to prevent herself from impulsively uttering the retort that sprang instantly to mind. He was telling her nicely, she reminded herself. She and Brynn both knew that conservative—dare she say drab?—garb was deemed the appropriate attire for Bradford Lipton's office. She should *not* tell Justin to take himself to the top of the Washington Monument and throw himself off.

She summoned a smile. "All right, Justin. I won't wear jeans to the office again, I promise." His warm smile and even warmer kiss were more than enough reward for her restraint. Stacey pressed closer to him and nuzzled his neck.

"Oh!"

Stacey and Justin both looked up at the sound of the startled exclamation.

"I'm terribly sorry! Excuse me! I—I sh-should have knocked!" Fred Rhodes stood on the threshold, his expression almost comical with shock.

"You certainly should have knocked, Freddie," Stacey agreed. She was about to rise from Justin's lap when he stood up abruptly, almost dumping her off. She clutched the side of the desk for support. Justin's face was fast becoming crimson.

Fred's face already was. "I—uh—had"—the man was totally nonplussed—"this memo." He waved a piece of paper before laying it down on the desk and backing slowly out the door. "Ex-Excuse me again. I'll just—er—go and —" He closed the door behind him.

"Uh-oh." Stacey grinned. "Guess who's going to be the topic of conversation around the office this afternoon?"

"It's not funny!" Justin was aghast. "Good Lord, he can't spread this all over the office!" He was gone from the office in a flash. To ensure Fred's silence, Stacey knew, although she didn't care who or what Fred told. But Justin did. It was a curiously painful realization that he was desperate to keep their affair a secret.

He returned a few minutes later, still somewhat shaken. "All taken care of," he said with a preoccupied air, and picked up the memo on his desk.

"What did you do, pull out his tongue?"

Justin didn't smile. He seemed not to have heard her. "Justin, what if everyone did find out that we're—er—having an affair? What do you suppose would happen?" Stacey dared to ask, holding her breath for his answer.

"Mmmph," was Justin's reply. He was studying the memo, his attention focused solely upon it. When he reached for the phone, his black eyes intent, she knew he'd forgotten all about her. The memo commanded his full concentration, and he was capable of shutting out everything but the issue at hand.

She sat down at her desk. There were several piles of index cards with names printed on them stacked on the desk, along with a note that instructed: Alphabetize. Stacey leafed through them. There must be close to four hundred cards, she thought. And she was to alphabetize them all? What a heinously tedious job! "Can I use a computer to do this?" she asked plaintively.

Justin did not reply. His chair was turned away from her and she could only see his back and hear his voice, deep and low, as he talked on the phone. She reached for the index cards.

Ten minutes later she gave up. There were seventy-six *A*s, she noted in dismay. And heaven only knows how many *B*s. And those were just the first two letters of the alphabet! With a quick glance at the back of Justin's head, she gathered up all the cards and left the office.

She strolled through the long, underground tunnel that connected the Senate Office Building to the House Office Building. The tunnel was filled with well-dressed office staffers, most of them young, walking briskly alone or in groups. Everyone seemed to have an air of purpose about them as they bustled through the underground corridor, and Stacey tried to inject a little purpose into her own stride.

Brynn worked on the House Human Resources Committee and shared an alcove with another staff member. She looked up when Stacey approached her desk. "Stace, hi! Back to work, hmm?"

"In a manner of speaking. They're inventing busywork for me. Can I borrow your terminal and put these names in alphabetical order?"

"Be my guest." Brynn obligingly gave Stacey her chair, then glanced at her watch. "A bunch of us are throwing a little birthday party for Lee Winters at one-thirty. We're holding it in the fourth-floor lounge. Care to join us?"

"Sure." Stacey smiled at the mention of the veteran congresswoman, who was well liked among the young staffers on the Hill. "Shall I chip in for the cake?"

"Give Marti a dollar when you see her." Brynn drifted off. Stacey turned her attention to the cards and typed the first name into the computer.

Eight

"Justin Marks would like to see you in his office immediately, Stacey," Diana Drew announced with a prim little smile the moment Stacey entered her father's office suite.

Stacey nodded and walked back to Justin's office.

"Where have you been?" was Justin's greeting to her when she opened the door.

She stepped inside, staring at him. His face was a taut, tense mask and his onyx eyes were cold and hard. "I—um—went over to Brynn's office to use her computer terminal." Stacey held up the completed alphabetized list. She was totally unprepared for Justin's display of anger. And for the first time, she shrank from it, rather than aggressively combating it with her own.

He snatched the list from her. "It's past three o'clock. Do you mean to tell me that it took you nearly three hours to feed those names into the computer?"

"It took half an hour. Then I ran some errands for Brynn and took a—uh—break."

"A break?" Justin roared. "You arrived at this office at noon. You did a half hour's work, then took a two-and-a-half-hour break?" He slammed the paper down on his desk. "I heard all about it,

Stacey. The wild noisy party in the fourth-floor lounge of the House Office Building. And you were right there, in the thick of it! Our office had an eye-witness call to report."

"Olive Mayer, that old battle-ax who works in Congressman Rawlings' office," Stacey surmised. "She looked self-righteously appalled when she looked in on us. The old bat can't stand to see any-one have a good time and she's terribly jealous of Lee Winters' staff. She—"

"The facts are, Stacey, that this is a workday afternoon," Justin interrupted coldly. "Every one of those revelers is being paid by the government to work, not to party. Furthermore, Miss Mayer said that the whole scene was one of utter debauchery, with people actually rolling around on the floor!"

"They were break-dancing," Stacey cried hotly. His anger had finally ignited her own temper. "A few of the pages were showing Lee Winters how it's done. It was a birthday party for Lee Winters, Justin. She's sixty years old today. There was cake and ginger ale and somebody turned on the radio. That was the entire debauched scene. I recall a similar bash in this very office the year my father turned fifty. Minus the break-dancing, of course."

Did Justin feel properly deflated? she wondered. Oh, she hoped so! But it was hard to tell by his sud-denly expressionless countenance. Finally, he cleared his throat. "Oh."

"Oh?" She glared at him. "That's all you have to say? Oh? After practically taking my head off? After accusing me of debauchery?"

He inhaled deeply, then firmly set his jaw. "You still had no business being over there, Stacey. You belong here where I—"

"Can keep an eagle eye on me so I won't do any-thing to embarrass my father?" Stacey picked up the computerized list, then threw it back down on the desk. "That's the main reason I'm here, isn't it, Justin? And if you can get a little sex on the side from the arrangement, well, so much the better for you!"

"Will you please lower your voice?" he said, his teeth clenched. "There is no need to—"

"No need to what, Justin? To announce to the staff that Senator Lipton's campaign manager laid the senator's daughter?" Her voice was shrill and she felt hot tears sting her eyes. This icy automaton was not her tender, passionate lover of the past few days. He wasn't the spontaneous man who had laughed at the lethargic pandas in the zoo and bought her a stuffed one more than half her height. The gentle, thoughtful man who stroked her hair and called her his darling had disappeared and left this uptight, condemning despot. He was back in his role of political pol where appearances were everything and hypocrisy was the order of the day.

"You've been on my case from the moment I walked into this office today!" she said hotly. "And when you weren't criticizing me, you ignored me completely. You're back to being the unfeeling, single-minded tyrant who is obsessed with—"

"That's not true!" he exclaimed. "Stacey, you know damn well how much I—"

"I know that having me here in this office is never going to work! I'll drive you crazy if you don't do it to me first. I quit, Justin! Brynn's job is secure and there is nothing else that you can do or say that will get me back into this office again!"

Thank heavens she hadn't told him about the baby, she thought miserably as she headed for the door. There had been so many times during the past two days when she'd been tempted to tell him, when she'd felt so close to him that telling him about their child had almost been a compulsion.

But, wary of his total immersion in the world of politics, she had resisted. And she'd been so right to do so!

"Stacey, you're not leaving!" Justin caught her arm and dragged her away from the door. "Sweetheart, we have to talk this out. I don't want to quarrel with you. I—"

"Let me go!" she howled. "We have nothing to talk about."

"Stacey, please, quiet down!" he said desperately. "In another minute we'll have the entire staff in here."

"It turns you into someone else!" she cried, trying wildly to break free. "This office. The image. The whole process! You're a different man here, Justin Marks, and I—we—" To her everlasting horror, she began to cry. Damn, she thought. She was so emotional, *too* emotional. All those hormones?

"Stacey, please don't cry!" Justin dropped her arm and began to pace the floor with increasing agitation.

He must be thoroughly exasperated with her, she decided unhappily. She was certainly exasperated with herself. It was so much easier to deal with anger than with tears. She had always ridiculed those foolish women who tried to manipulate others with their weeping. But she wasn't trying to manipulate Justin. She was in pain—and confused and frightened as well. "It's no use." She tried frantically to brush away the tears with her hands. She'd known all along that a relationship between Justin and herself was hopeless. But facing it hurt so much! "It's just no use," she sobbed softly.

"What's no use? Stacey, *please* don't cry. I admit that I came down too hard on you about that party, but . . ." He reached into his coat pocket and pulled out a pristine white handkerchief and handed it to her. "Honey, Olive Mayer *is* a self-righteous, condemning prig. And though I knew you wouldn't be involved in anything—er—debauched, having to listen to that old crone gossip, realizing that she'd be spreading her tales, embellishing everything to anyone who would listen, simply infuriated me. I admit I overreacted, Stacey." He stopped pacing and extended his hand to her. "And I was jealous as hell. Mayer said you were dancing with—"

"She was certainly embellishing that time, Justin," she interrupted him, ignoring the hand he offered to her. "I wasn't dancing with anyone. But you didn't bother to ask me, did you? You simply assumed the worst and jumped down my throat for it because preserving the Lipton image is everything to you and any threats to defile it are tantamount to a war crime in your mind!"

"I'm sorry." He moved to stand directly in front of her, so close that she need only step a few inches to be in his arms. Stacey did not take the necessary step. She remained stiff and unyielding, and Justin heaved a heavy sigh. "It was stupid of me to let Olive Mayer goad me into attacking you. My only excuse is that this has been one hell of a day, Stacey. After being away from the office for two days, I have an in-basket stacked to overflowing and at least seventy-five phone calls to return and—" He reached out to touch her still wet cheek. "I didn't want to fight with you, Stacey. And I certainly didn't mean to make you cry."

She turned away from him. Perhaps he didn't mean to, but he had. Because all his thoughts and energies were directed into his political ambitions and everything—every*one*—else was secondary. She'd seen it with her father all her life. Bradford Lipton wasn't a malicious person. He didn't mean to hurt his family, but he did, constantly, through his omissions. The senator was unavailable and preoccupied, which made him remote and insensitive to his family, who were not similarly consumed by his political career. And with Justin, it was simply more of the same.

"I'm going home now, Justin." There was no reason for her to stay.

"No!" he said fiercely, and moved to block the door. "Stacey, I'm not going to let you—"

The telephone rang, and for Stacey it was a most welcome interruption. "Wait!" Justin said as he picked up the phone, and the uncharacteristic plea in the voice that usually snapped out orders, caused her to pause on the threshold.

And then: *"He what?"* Justin's voice exploded like a blast from a cannon. "No, the senator has no comment at this time. We will release a statement later in the day. No, I have no comment on the subject. I feel it would be inappropriate to comment on the matter at this point in time."

Stacey recognized the look on his face and the tone of voice. What had one of her brothers done now? she wondered. Justin placed the receiver in its cradle with a thud. His dark eyes were stormy. "What happened?" she asked, her curiosity overcoming her desire to escape.

"An interview with your brother Lucas was published in the campus newspaper yesterday." Justin's nostrils flared. They really did. She wouldn't have been surprised to see steam come forth when he exhaled.

"And today," he went on, "some of his more memorable remarks were reprinted in the local paper in town, where some sharpie pointed out certain comments to the wire services." Justin picked up a pencil and snapped it in two. "The story will appear in all the papers throughout the country by tomorrow morning."

Stacey's eyes widened. National news coverage for Lucas? That sounded ominous. "What did Lucas say?" she dared to ask.

"Oh, the boy said quite a few things. When asked what he liked to do in his leisure time when not playing football, Lucas Lipton was quoted as saying that he liked to drink beer, shoot pool, and"—Justin's voice rose—"expletive deleted girls! Except he didn't delete the expletive!"

Stacey could just hear Lucas say it in that jovial, bad-boy way of his. She laughed.

It was a major mistake. Justin positively glowered at her. "It's not funny!" he thundered. "Do you realize his remarks will be aired in the national press? And it's just the sort of anecdote that the network newscasters like to throw in at the end of their broadcasts. The son of the upright senator who espouses all the traditional morals and values likes to—"

"Oh, Justin, you're overreacting again. Lucas is a college kid, and a football player too. His answer won't shock anyone. It's what they'd expect of him. Everybody knows darn well that a good-looking college jock's pastimes aren't going to be making fudge and playing with toy trains."

"Why couldn't he have *said* they were!" Justin groaned. "You're underestimating the seriousness of the situation, Stacey. The liberal press is hostile to your father. Their own media darling is Whit Chambers, and anything—*anything*—derogatory that they can pin on Bradford Lipton is maximized to the nth degree. Our polls show that your father's message is reaching the people, but it's an uphill struggle against those piranhas of the press. And what we didn't need the week that the senator announces his candidacy is for his son to announce that he is a beer-drinking, pool-shooting—"

"Expletive-deleter of girls," finished Stacey. Justin got so wrapped up in every trivial detail, she thought. It was what made him an invaluable aide, but it would also contribute to ulcers, high blood pressure, and heaven knows what else. A sense of humor was essential, a lifesaver. She smiled at him, hoping to bring forth a similar response.

Justin threw up his hands, his frustration obvious. "I might have known you would find the whole incident hilarious." He headed for the door, scowling. "Sterne and Spence will probably be rolling with laughter too. Sometimes I think the four of you *work* at coming up with politically embarrassing remarks. Sometimes I think you're all on the payroll of the opposition!"

She heard him in the corridor, calling the staff together to discuss the latest gaffe and to prepare a suitable statement for the soon-to-be-clamoring press. He'd left her without a single backward glance.

Stacey decided to go home. There was certainly nothing for her to do here. And the sight of any one of the errant Lipton offspring at this particular time was liable to make the senator's staff foam at the mouth. She drove back to her apartment, depression weighing heavily upon her. The idyll with Justin was indeed over. The closeness was gone and they stood on opposite sides, unable even to see the other's point of view, totally separated by the unbreachable gulf of politics.

Back in her apartment, she made herself a cup of tea and sat down to drink it, hoping to soothe her shattered spirits. Everything was moving too quickly. Her mind was whirling with confusion, compounded by fear. Justin . . . the baby . . . the campaign . . . Her thoughts tumbled through her head like pieces in a kaleidoscope, and the images she saw differed every time. What was the right thing to do? And how would she know to do it?

When the doorbell rang, Stacey assumed that Brynn had forgotten her key. She was a little early, but perhaps she'd managed to catch all the green lights, an extremely rare occurrence. So certain was she that it was her roommate, she didn't bother to glance through the peephole, her usual habit before opening the door. Instead she flung open the door and found herself facing . . . Cord Marshall?

Stacey groaned inwardly. Marshall was probably furious that Justin had canceled her appearance on his show tomorrow. No doubt he was there to try to talk her into coming on anyway. She had no intention of doing so and mentally geared herself for the upcoming unpleasant scene.

"Hello, Stacey." Marshall smiled. "I'm glad I found you at home."

She stared at him. Cord Marshall didn't look furious, yet his smile chilled her. He somehow reminded her of a shark circling an unsuspecting swimmer. "What do you want, Mr. Marshall?" She did not invite him inside.

"Cord," he corrected smoothly. "I've come to discuss your appearance on my show tomorrow night, Stacey."

She sighed. "I'm sure you received the message from Justin Marks this morning canceling it, Mr. Marsh—uh—Cord."

"I didn't want to involve Marks in our little secret, Stacey." Marshall's smile never wavered. "But unless you agree to be on the show, I'll have no choice but to tell him about this." With a rather dramatic flourish, he withdrew a bent-up box from the folds of his raincoat.

Stacey gasped and clutched the door for support.

It was the box that had contained her pregnancy-testing kit!

"Beautiful!" Cord Marshall said with a pleased laugh. "A completely spontaneous, uninhibited reaction. I'd guessed it was yours because I observed your near faint during your father's announcement, but there was always the chance it might have belonged to your hellcat of a roommate. You just confirmed my hunch, though, angel face. You're pregnant—and you haven't got a husband to share the good news with."

"You got that box out of the garbage!" Stacey cried. "Brynn mentioned that she'd found you skulking around the building several days ago. You went scrounging through our garbage cans like a—a rat!"

Marshall shrugged. "I like to call it investigative reporting. Sometimes I find nothing on the old garbage route, but more often than not there's some little gem tucked away. What a person throws away can be extremely revealing, Stacey."

"You're vile! Justin said you were a garbage-scrounger! He knows how low you would stoop for a story!"

"What he *doesn't* know is that you're pregnant, eh, Stacey? I'd venture to guess no one knows except that red-haired spitfire you have for a roommate. And now me, of course. Who's the father?"

"That's none of your business!"

"Relax, doll, I'm not going to press you." Marshall smiled again, and Stacey longed to wipe that smug expression off his face—along with the rest of his features! "I happen to revere expectant mothers. A sort of Madonna complex, I suppose. I have no intention of exposing your little secret. I merely intend to blackmail you with it."

"Oh!" Stacey felt a wave of dizziness sweep over her. The man was literally making her sick.

"Sweetie, try to remain calm. A mother's moods can affect that little person within, you know." Marshall had the nerve to look concerned. "You'll find my demands extremely easy to meet. Simply appear on my show tomorrow night for a fifteen-minute segment and I'll forget all about the little guy or doll you're carrying. You have my word of honor, Stacey."

"You have no honor! You're a blackmailer and a garbage-scrounger and a—"

"Let's not resort to name-calling, Stacey. Why not deal on a strictly business level? I need to fill fifteen minutes of my show tomorrow night with a human-interest story that will appeal to my female viewers. The daughter of a newly announced presidential candidate fits the bill. I *promise* not to mention a word about your . . . delicate condition, Stacey. I swear on my sainted grandmother's grave that I won't. Look at it this way, you can actually help your father by appearing. Be sweet, be funny, turn on the charm! You could garner your daddy lots of votes."

"I can't!" she said, distraught. "Justin said it was out of the question. He'll kill me if I appear on your show!"

"The bully!" Marshall sniffed. "Stacey, you have nothing to fear. We'll talk about whatever you want to discuss. You'll be on the air for less than fifteen minutes with time out for commercials."

"What about the daughters of the other candidates?"

"None of them had the courtesy to even return my calls. It has to be you, Stacey."

What was she going to do? She suppressed the urge to scream for help. She was trapped and she knew it. "If I refuse to appear . . ." She gulped. She had to hear him say the words.

He said them. "I'll announce your out-of-wedlock pregnancy on the air. That's a promise, Stacey."

It was a threat, and an extremely effective one. White and silent, Stacey clung to the door.

"Be at the studio at six-thirty," Marshall said. "We go on the air at seven and you'll be on first. Good-bye, Stacey." He started down the stairs, whistling a jaunty tune.

"What are *you* doing here?" Stacey heard Brynn's voice on the stairwell. The whistling stopped abruptly. "We spray against fungus in this building, Marshall." Brynn sounded as threatening as Cagney or Lacey on a bust.

"P-Put that away!" Cord Marshall sounded very nervous.

"You'd better run, Marshall!" Brynn warned. "Run fast!" There was the sound of running footsteps echoing heavily throughout the stairwell. Brynn appeared at the door moments later with her purse-size spray can of Mace in her hand. She took one look at Stacey's face and muttered, "I should have blasted him. What was Marshall doing here, Stace?"

Stacey haltingly told her of Marshall's threats. "You can't let him blackmail you, Stacey!" Brynn was outraged. "Call Justin and tell him everything. Let *him* deal with Marshall!"

"Tell Justin?" Stacey exclaimed, aghast. "I can't do that, Brynn. I'd rather appear on *The Cord Marshall Show*."

"Stacey, you and Justin aren't enemies anymore. You're in love, remember?"

Justin's face as she had last seen him—furious, exasperated, disgusted—flashed painfully through Stacey's mind. "I'm sure he's had second thoughts about that, Brynn."

"In a single day?" Brynn said scoffingly. "No way."

"Oh, yes, Brynnie. During the two days Justin wasn't involved in the campaign everything was wonderful between us. More than wonderful. But it all ended today, the moment he set foot back in the office. It just will never work between us." She ran her hand through her hair, tousling it. "Cord Marshall promised he wouldn't mention the baby. Maybe it won't be so bad doing the show. Maybe I can garner some votes for Dad. Maybe Justin won't even find out that I was on the show!"

Brynn rolled her eyes heavenward. "Maybe Prince Charles will dump Princess Di and marry Tina Turner. Come on, Stace, face reality!"

"I can't tell Justin, Brynn!" Stacey wailed. "If you could've seen his face when he heard what Lucas said to some campus reporter . . ."

"About drinking beer, shooting pool, and—uh—dating girls?" Brynn flashed a grin. "I heard it on the radio driving home from work. The DJ was very jocularly quoting Lucas."

So the jokes had started already. Stacey sucked in her breath. "Dad hates to be the object of jokes, even more than he hates to be criticized. He'll be livid. And when Dad is upset, Justin goes into orbit. I don't dare drop this bombshell on him now!"

Justin couldn't possibly love her after she'd made an appearance on Cord Marshall's show in direct opposition to his wishes, she thought. But if she didn't go on the show, Marshall would announce her pregnancy *on the air*! And if Lucas's college-boy remarks could cause trouble for her father, imagine what the news of his unmarried daughter's pregnancy would do! Stacey shuddered. She decided that this was the worst day of her life. "I have to go on that show, Brynn."

"I suppose you really don't have much of a choice." Brynn nodded glumly. "But you don't have to face that barracuda alone, Stacey. I'll go to the studio with you. And, who knows, maybe it *won't* be so bad, after all."

Stacey walked off the sound stage and covered her face with her hands. Brynn was waiting in the wings, and she draped a comforting arm around Stacey's shoulders.

"It was a disaster!" Stacey murmured. "Oh, why am I so awful at interviews? No wonder Justin never lets me do any!"

"It wasn't all that bad," Brynn said loyally. "I mean, your dad may not be thrilled that you told Marshall that he likes to swim in the nude, but it's no great scandal, Stace."

"I don't know why I said it." Stacey shook her head woefully. "Marshall was talking about certain presidents swimming nude in the White House pool and the next thing I knew . . ."

"Marshall is very sneaky. He led you right into it," Brynn said indignantly.

"Brynnie, when he started talking about White House weddings, I absolutely panicked. I was sure he was going to make some reference to—" Stacey's hand unconsciously touched her abdomen. "I hardly knew what I was saying after that."

"He took advantage of you, the slime!"

"I actually told him about the time Mom and I dropped in on Sterne and found a blonde handcuffed to the taps of his bathtub." Stacey's voice was barely a squeak. "I said it on the air!"

Brynn grimaced. "Marshall tricked you, Stace. He was trying to intimate that your family is feuding with Sterne because his apartment is off limits to everyone. You just—er—explained why."

"Justin will never forgive me," Stacey whispered.

"Well, at least you made it clear that there's no

real family feud. I thought it was beautiful when you said that you Liptons accept each other no matter how bizarre your behavior. If only Marshall hadn't jumped in to ask what other bizarre behavior your family indulged in."

"I told him I refused to discuss it." Stacey bit her lower lip. "I guess that wasn't such a great answer, either."

"Well, let's look on the bright side," Brynn said bracingly. "The interview is over and Marshall didn't mention a word about the baby."

"Mr. Marshall!" A worried-looking young stagehand motioned to Cord Marshall, who was still on the sound stage. A filmstrip was being aired and Marshall slipped quietly from his chair and joined them in the wings. "What is it, Joe?" he asked the stagehand. He winked rakishly at Stacey and Brynn. They did not wink back.

"Your dressing room, sir. There was a terrible odor seeping out into the hall, so I went in to investigate." The stagehand made a face. "The smell is abominable. Like something is rotting or decaying, only worse."

"Damn, let's check it out, Joe," Marshall said, and he and the younger man disappeared from view.

"Let's go, Stace," suggested Brynn, and Stacey gave a dejected nod.

"Dammit!" Cord Marshall's bellow could be heard throughout the studio. He emerged from his dressing room carrying a handful of bottles, his face almost purple with rage. "Somebody poured five bottles of skunk oil all over my dressing room! The place reeks! It's uninhabitable!"

"Not for a skunk," Brynn said sweetly. "I'd say it was a fitting habitat for you, Mr. Marshall."

Stacey's eyes widened. "Brynn, did you—"

Cord Marshall reached the same conclusion. "You did it, you red-haired she-devil!" he raged.

"Brynn." Stacey grabbed her arm. "I think it's time we were leaving." The two took off down the hall.

"I'll get you, you little fiend!" Marshall was hot on their trail. "I've got a long score to settle with you! I'm going to make you sorry you were ever born."

They gained a little time when Marshall tripped over a cable that Stacey and Brynn had nimbly avoided. He went sprawling onto the ground and the two women rushed from the building.

"Brynn, where did you get skunk oil?" Stacey gasped as they started toward her BMW parked in a nearby lot.

"I called every novelty shop in Washington till I found it—although rat poison was my first choice. Stace, we're safe!"

Except that they weren't. For climbing out of his gray Oldsmobile was Justin Marks, his face a mask of unholy rage. He spotted Stacey and Brynn immediately, before they saw him. "Stacey!" His voice caused them to freeze in their tracks.

"Come here, Stacey." Justin's voice was hard and deadly calm. Stacey's heart, already pounding from the exertion of the chase, tripled its tempo. "Don't make me come over there to fetch you, Stacey." The controlled fury of his voice was infinitely more chilling than Cord Marshall's raving bellows.

Which suddenly sounded from the building. "There she is!" Marshall ran out into the parking lot, accompanied by the stagehand, another man, and a woman. "The maniacal redhead! Get her!"

Stacey and Brynn had time to exchange horrified glances before simultaneously making a wild dash to the car. They jumped in, locked both doors, and Stacey had just inserted her key in the ignition when Justin appeared beside her window, at almost the precise moment Cord Marshall reached Brynn's side of the car.

"What now, Stace?" cried Brynn.

Stacey put the car in reverse and pressed the gas pedal to the floor. The car shot backward, leaving a startled and furious Justin and an equally disturbed Cord Marshall staring after it.

Neither Brynn nor Stacey uttered a word until they were safely launched in the anonymity of the Beltway traffic.

"I thought we were in a horror movie for a few minutes there," Brynn said at last, her voice shaky. "With Godzilla at one window and the Swamp Beast at the other. You were terrific, Stace," she added admiringly. "You drove like Mario Andretti at the Indy 500."

Stacey made no reply. Her heart had finally resumed its normal rhythm and she was able to breathe without gasping. "I don't think we'd better go back to the apartment tonight, Brynn," she said at last. "And my parents' house is out too."

"And we'd better steer clear of Sterne's infamous apartment. We've had enough excitement for one night."

"Let's drive down to Spence and Patty's farm in Fredericksburg." Stacey steered the car into the lane directing travelers to Virginia. "It's only ninety minutes away and no one would think to look for us there." Justin and the senator gave Spence and Patty a wide berth. "We could spend the rest of the weekend with them."

Brynn brightened. "And by Monday, things will have calmed down." She gulped. "I hope."

Nine

Nothing ever seemed to faze Spence and Patty Lipton. When Stacey and Brynn arrived on their doorstep shortly after nine, the couple ushered them inside their old farmhouse without comment, as if the women's sudden appearance and request for sanctuary were entirely commonplace.

Spence offered them the extra room adjacent to the bedroom where the three children were sleeping, and Patty served wild strawberry tea and slabs of homemade bread. Though they asked no questions, Stacey felt obliged to explain their impromptu arrival. "I was on *The Cord Marshall Show* tonight," she told them as she sipped her tea.

"Oh, I get it!" Spence flashed a devilish grin. "You need someplace to hide out while the heat's on. Should we be expecting Justin Marks with a bullhorn, a SWAT team, and tear gas?"

Brynn grimaced wryly. "After what we've been through tonight, that isn't as far-fetched as it might seem." She and Stacey took turns relating the events of the evening. Spence and Patty were delighted with the tale.

"Although I don't think you should do much running in your condition, Stacey," Spence remarked with a thoughtful frown. "Patty believes that pregnancy shouldn't limit a woman's activities at all, but I think an expectant mother should take it a bit easier, especially in the first and last trimesters."

The piece of bread Stacey had been munching on fell soundlessly from her fingers to the floor. Brynn inhaled her tea and promptly choked.

"How—how did you know?" Stacey managed to ask after Brynn had stopped choking and was breathing normally again.

"We hadn't seen you for a while before your father's announcement," Patty said calmly. "Spence noticed the change in you right away. When you nearly fainted in the Senate Caucus Room . . ." She shrugged. "We just knew."

"When's your due date? Of course, you'll have natural childbirth, there's no other way." Spence beamed at Stacey. "Have you thought of any names? Patty and I have a terrific book of unusual names we can lend you. Oh, who's the father?"

"Oh, Spencer, the father is Justin Marks." Patty smiled serenely.

Spence nearly dropped his teacup in a display of uncharacteristic surprise. Stacey and Brynn gaped at Patty, equally stunned. "Who else could it be?" Patty said, shrugging, as if that explained it all.

"It's true," Stacey whispered, staring from Patty to Spence in wide-eyed wonder. "But he doesn't know."

"Justin Marks!" Spence seemed unable to comprehend it. "Justin Marks?"

"They've been in love with each other for years," Patty said. "It's obvious their karmic destinies are intertwined. But they had to wait until their ruling planets were favorably aligned."

"Of course." Spence nodded, as if *that* explained it all.

Stacey and Brynn exchanged glances.

"Have you seen a doctor, Stacey?" asked Spence.

She shook her head. "I intend to, soon, but . . ."

"I understand," Patty said. "I know how cold and aloof doctors can be." She patted Stacey's shoulder. "While you're here you must meet Kimberly, the midwife who delivered our babies." Her face glowed with enthusiasm. "She's wonderful. Experienced and warm and understanding. A firm believer in home deliveries and—"

"A midwife named Kimberly?" interrupted Brynn.

Spence nodded happily. "Call her tonight, Patty. Set up an appointment for Stacey to see her tomorrow."

"What a wonderful idea!" Patty was on her feet, heading for the old black phone in the kitchen.

"But—" Stacey began.

"You can deliver here, Stace." Spence smiled broadly. "Patty and I will assist Kimberly with the birth. And would you mind if the children watch their new cousin being born? What a moving and spiritually enlightening experience that will be for them!"

Kimberly, a slim blonde somewhere in her late twenties, did not fit Stacey's image of a rural midwife at all. But the sight of her nursing school degree and certificate from a university midwifery program, framed and hanging on her office wall, boosted Stacey's confidence somewhat.

The young midwife proved to be exactly as Patty had described her—experienced and understanding, friendly and warm. She performed the examination with professional expertise. "Are you absolutely certain of the date you conceived?"

Kimberly asked as they sat in her small living room after the examination.

"Absolutely." Stacey thought back to that hot August night. "It was the only possible time."

Kimberly nodded. "Then I'm going to recommend that we have a sonogram done at the hospital this afternoon. Stacey, the size of your uterus is significantly larger than it would normally be for a single pregnancy of this duration."

"What?" Stacey stared at her, uncomprehending.

"Stacey." Kimberly took her hands and held them in her own. "I think you should prepare yourself for the possibility that you're carrying twins."

"Twins!" Brynn repeated for the thousandth time as she drove Stacey's car back to Washington late Sunday afternoon. Stacey sat in the front seat beside her, unable to drive, unable to think coherently, unable to do anything but repeat after Brynn, "Twins!"

They'd all trooped to the hospital together— Brynn, Spence, Patty, the three little girls, Stacey, and Kimberly—and everyone had crowded into the small room where the sonogram visually confirmed Kimberly's prediction. Twins.

Stacey had been in a daze ever since.

"Stace, you're going to have to tell . . . someone!" Brynn was a nervous wreck. She'd bitten off eight of her hard-grown fingernails since hearing the news. "I mean two! You—we—can't manage this on our own any longer. At least tell your mother, Stacey."

"Brynnie, Mother will never understand! She'll hate me!" Stacey cried out, anguished.

"You said the same thing the time we skipped school in junior high to go to the movies and got caught. But when you told her, she *did* understand and she didn't hate you. She even told you about the time she'd skipped school and gotten caught. Remember?"

"Brynn, you can't compare a childish transgression to a situation like this! As an adult, my mother has always been perfect. She's always done everything correctly. She'll never understand, Brynnie! She'll hate me!"

"Stacey." Brynn bit off nail number nine. "Tell your mother."

Stacey sat in the beautifully decorated living room of the Lipton home, her hands balled into fists, her eyes downcast. Brynn had dropped her off at the house and driven back to the apartment.

"Oh, Stacey!" her mother had said when she'd blurted out the news. Caroline Lipton paced the living room, lithe and lovely and undeniably distressed. "Oh, my poor little girl!" She sat down on the sofa beside Stacey and took one of Stacey's hands in both of hers. Stacey looked up to see tears swimming in her mother's wide-set, light brown eyes. "My poor little Stacey." Caroline's voice quavered. "You must be terrified. You must feel so alone and confused . . . and guilty too."

Stacey swallowed the boulder that had lodged in her throat. Her heart was pounding as loudly as a tympanic drum. "Yes," she whispered. "That's exactly the way I feel, Mom."

"I know, honey." Caroline squeezed Stacey's hand. "You see, I've been through it, Stacey. The circumstances differed slightly—I was twenty-one years old and pregnant with just one baby. But . . . I was unmarried and terrified to tell my family and the baby's father. I know exactly what you're going through right now, Stacey."

Stacey could only stare at her, her mouth agape. "Mother!" she gasped at last. "You?"

Caroline hugged her close. "The baby was you, Stacey, and the man was your father."

Stacey was absolutely floored. Her upstanding, conservative father and her poised, perfect mother *had* to get married? She gave her head a shake as if to clear it. It couldn't be true! She was having an extremely peculiar dream and would awaken at any moment.

"Your father was perfectly wonderful when I finally gathered up my courage and told him. He insisted that we be married right away, and we were. We did alter the date by a few months, though." Caroline smiled faintly. "Brad thought that it wouldn't do for the child of a congressman from Nebraska to be born just seven months after the wedding ceremony." Her smile deepened. "We've been so happy, Stacey. We've had a perfectly wonderful marriage."

Stacey drew back to stare at her incredulously. "You have?"

"Oh, yes. Your father and I are as much in love today as"—Caroline gave a little laugh—"as the night you were conceived, Stacey. Oh, it was hard on me when you children were small, with Brad away so much and me at home. Since you've all grown up, I've been able to become more active, even to campaign on my own. Daddy and I have never been happier, Stacey."

"You like politics," Stacey said slowly.

"I guess I'm basically a bit of a ham." Caroline's cheeks pinked becomingly. "But, Stacey, I love everything about the political life. The attention, the limelight, the crowds and excitement. I'd go mad with the humdrum existence of a husband working some dull nine-to-five job."

Stacey listened, awed, as her lifetime perceptions were overturned one by one. Her mother loved her life in the political arena. Her marriage had been no sacrifice at all. She was completely satisfied with it. And she was glad her mother was happy and not trapped living a lifestyle that she loathed.

As I would be, Stacey thought bleakly. Her mother's words hadn't changed her own attitudes at all. What Caroline Lipton loved about the political life, Stacey hated. She craved that humdrum existence with a husband working a job with regular hours, the life her mother scorned.

Telling her mother who was the father of her unborn babies was easy compared to confessing her pregnancy. And Caroline was delighted. "Justin is such a steady, reliable man. So loyal, so hard-working. And what an interesting angle for the press—the campaign manager is the candidate's son-in-law!"

Bradford Lipton arrived home an hour later and was told the news by his wife, at Stacey's request. He came into Stacey's old bedroom a few minutes later, obviously uncomfortable and ill at ease. Such emotional moments were not Bradford Lipton's forte. The man who could face a crowd of thousands without losing his cool was clearly out of his element as he faced his only daughter. "I want you to know that I am not condemning you, Stacey," he murmured, staring fixedly at the carpet. "A woman . . . a man . . ." His face reddened. "Your mother and I both understand."

Stacey had to smile. In that moment, she regretted that she and her father were emotional strangers and probably always would be. Bradford Lipton was close to no one, except, perhaps, his wife.

"Thank you, Dad," she said quietly. Her father was being remarkably kind, she thought. He hadn't said a word about the possible effects of public reaction on his campaign.

"I'm very pleased you'll be marrying Justin, Stacey." The senator's voice warmed as he called downstairs to his wife. "Caroline, why don't you arrange the wedding for tomorrow? The—er—sooner, the better, eh?"

"Tomorrow?" echoed Stacey, paling.

"Fine, darling." Caroline appeared at the door and smiled at her husband. "We'll have a private ceremony with only the family present. And Grace and Brynn, of course. I'll begin making arrangements tonight."

Stacey listened in horror. "Mom, Dad, I'd better talk this over with Justin first." Her stomach lurched at the thought. Justin was furious with her. To the point of hating her? He'd last seen her Saturday night when she'd nearly run him over with her car. And now her parents were planning to marry her off to him, without his knowledge.

"Mrs. Lipton," Grace called from the downstairs vestibule. "Justin Marks is here to see the senator."

"He has a remarkable sense of timing, doesn't he, Caroline?" A smiling Bradford Lipton started down the stairs, followed by his wife, her face aglow. Stacey remained in the bedroom, unable to move. She heard all the voices.

Her father's booming, "Welcome to the family, Justin. I assure you that Caroline and I are pleased."

Her mother's breathless, "We *are* delighted, Justin. Bradford and I want to have the wedding here tomorrow night. You and Stacey needn't concern yourselves with the details. I'll be happy to handle everything."

And finally, Justin's bewildered, "Wedding?"

"Stacey, dear," Caroline called in a sweetly melodious voice. "Justin is here."

Stacey walked slowly down the stairs. So this was the way the soldiers felt when they landed on the beaches of Normandy on D day, she thought. She paused on the last step and surveyed the group. Her handsome, charismatic father, her beautiful, radiant mother. And a thoroughly bewildered and somewhat apprehensive Justin Marks.

"Ah, here is the bride!" Her father extended his hand to her. "I'm sure you two want to be alone. You have so much to discuss."

Stacey and Justin stared at each other. Her first date hadn't been this awkward, Stacey thought glumly. What on earth could she say to the man after this?

"Would you like to go for a drive?" Justin asked in a tense, tight voice.

"No!" she exclaimed, then glanced at her parents. "Thank you, I'd rather not," she added politely.

"A romantic drive through Rock Creek Park!" the senator said heartily. "Brings back memories, doesn't it, Caroline? You two young people just run along now. Have fun."

Justin took Stacey's arm in a grip as tight as a blood-pressure cuff and led her from the house without a word. Stacey shivered, but not from the nighttime chill in the air.

"Your parents seem to believe that you've accepted my proposal," Justin said tautly as he steered the gray Olds along the tree-lined streets. "How did they reach that conclusion, Stacey?"

Tell him, a voice inside her head screamed. Tell him before it gets even worse.

"Not talking to me?" His voice was cold and rapier-sharp. "My arrival at that given moment was quite inconvenient for you, wasn't it, Stacey?

You hadn't expected to be caught up in your lie so quickly."

She moved her lips to speak, but the words wouldn't come. He was angry with her, so terribly angry.

"You rejected my proposal," he continued icily. "You only wanted an affair with me, remember?"

He sounded hurt, she realized, and her heart ached for him. She'd hurt him when she'd refused to marry him and she hadn't even been aware of it.

"My proposal is withdrawn, Stacey. An affair is all you want from me and that's all you'll get. And you had no right to concoct some piece of fiction involving me to get you off the hook with your parents. Tomorrow you're going to tell them the truth, Stacey."

The truth. She swallowed hard. Justin didn't know the full truth. He was hurt and angry. He thought that she'd used him for her own ends, to escape the consequences of her appearance on *The Cord Marshall Show*. But how could she tell him the whole truth now, when he was so cold, so angry?

"I deeply resent your trying to divert your father's anger over your appearance on that abominable television show by telling him that we're getting married. It was cowardly and deceitful, Stacey. Not to mention malicious!"

"It didn't happen that way," she said softly. A covert glance at his unyielding profile brought a sudden rush of tears to her eyes. He hated her, she thought. He really did. He said he'd *withdrawn his proposal*! And her mother was undoubtedly arranging their wedding this very moment. Stacey's hand rested lightly on her abdomen. *Two* babies were growing within her. Justin's children. If she were to tell him, she knew he would dutifully marry her, even though he'd come to loathe her.

She remembered the brief days they'd spent together in loving harmony, when the promise of a deep and abiding love had been an actuality, not a shattered dream. But it was hopeless now.

"Don't worry, Justin," she said around the constriction in her throat. "We're not getting married."

He pulled the car to a stop in front of her apartment building. "Kindly inform your parents of that fact." He didn't glance at her. He kept his eyes fixed firmly ahead as she quickly climbed out of the car.

"Stacey, what happened?" cried Brynn as she watched Stacey haphazardly toss clothes into her suitcase. "What are you doing? Where are you going?"

"I'm going to live with Spence and Patty. We'll be in relative obscurity down on the farm. Kimberly can deliver the babies and—and my little nieces can watch and . . ."

"Good Lord, you've flipped! Stacey, what did your parents say? Are they going to disown you or what? Please, please talk to me!"

"They expect me to marry Justin tomorrow night, Brynn. And he doesn't want to marry me, he can't stand me! Oh, it's just no use, Brynnie. Our—our planets aren't favorably aligned after all."

"Ohh!" Brynn groaned.

"I have to go. I have to get out of Washington." Stacey gave Brynn a quick, hard hug. "I'll call you when—"

"Stacey, I'm not letting you drive down to that farm alone at night in the state you're in. If you insist on going, I'm going with you."

"But you have to be at work tomorrow, Brynn."

"I'll call the office and tell them I'm taking a few

vacation days. Stacey, won't you please reconsider and talk this over with Justin?"

"We've already talked, Brynn. It's hopeless." Stacey blinked back her tears. She would *not* cry again. She must direct all her thoughts and energies to her new life. Crying over what might have been was demoralizing and useless.

Brynn pulled her suitcase out of the closet. "I just hope Spence doesn't expect us to milk that evil-looking cow of his. Or tangle with that macho rooster, either," she added grimly.

Ten

Stacey, Brynn, and the three little girls sat at the kitchen table of the old farmhouse the next morning, playing with a flour-and-water dough Patty had whipped up earlier.

"No, Aurora, we don't eat it." Stacey retrieved some dough from the two-year-old's mouth for the fifteenth time. "We play with it. It's play dough."

"She eats the store kind too," said Sunshine. "Look at the kitty cat I made, Aunt Stacey."

Stacey smiled. "He's adorable, Sunny."

"When Mommy and Daddy coming home?" demanded three-year-old Melody. Patty and Spence had driven into town for supplies an hour earlier.

"Very soon." Brynn cocked her head to one side. "In fact, I think I hear a car coming up the road now."

The three children tore out of the kitchen, squealing with anticipation. "It's not Daddy and Mommy," came Sunny's disappointed voice. "It's Justin Marks."

"Stace, don't panic," Brynn said quickly. But Stacey did just that. She snatched Patty's thick woolen sweater from a hook on the wall and dashed out the kitchen door.

Justin found her in the hayloft of the barn fifteen minutes later. "Will you come down?" he asked quietly, standing at the bottom of the wooden ladder and looking up at her. "Or shall I come up?"

"Neither. Go away!"

He put his foot on the lowest rung of the ladder. "Not until I recite the speech I've been rehearsing the whole way down here."

"I don't want to hear it. I hate speeches."

"I know." He began to climb slowly, steadily, up the ladder. "I called your apartment a half hour after I dropped you off last night, Stacey. And when there was no answer, I drove over only to find you and Brynn had gone. One of your neighbors said he'd seen the two of you leave with suitcases."

Stacey couldn't stand the suspense a moment longer. "How did you know we were here, Justin? Why are *you* here?" She felt sick with apprehension. "Do you . . . know?" she whispered.

He was standing midway up the ladder and was on eye level with her. "Patty called me this morning. She mentioned something about ruling houses and signs and planets." He gave a slight laugh. "I didn't understand, but then, that's nothing out of the ordinary. I seldom understand what Patty is talking about."

He deftly climbed into the loft and sat down beside her in the hay. Stacey allowed herself to cast a quick glance at him. He was wearing his tan cords, a white shirt, and his new blue sweater. She quickly looked away when she felt his gaze upon her.

He reached out awkwardly to touch the bright calico dress she was wearing, one of Patty's maternity dresses. "You look pretty," he said hoarsely.

Stacey was trembling. "Justin, did Patty tell you I'm—"

"You tell me, Stacey."

She took a deep breath. This was it. "I'm pregnant." The words tumbled out before she dared to think about what she was saying. "With twins. That night in August . . ."

He was reaching for her. Stacey saw the sympathy and concern in his eyes and she couldn't bear it. She scrambled away from him, moving deeper into the loft. "I don't want your pity, Justin. I don't need it. And you don't have to marry me. I can—"

"Stacey, of course I'm going to marry you."

"No!" She kept backing away from him. "You don't want to. You withdrew your proposal and I—I don't blame you, Justin. We'd be impossible together and we both know it."

He pounced as swiftly and as lithely as a barnyard cat. In a disorienting second, Stacey found herself lying in the hay with Justin on top of her. He held her hands above her head and laced his fingers with hers. "Stacey," he said huskily, gazing into her tawny-brown eyes. "Oh, my darling!"

"No, Justin," she pleaded as his lips lightly brushed her own. "Oh, please, no!" When he looked at her that way, when he touched her, she couldn't think. And she must keep a clear head. She had to!

"I came back last night to reinstate my proposal." He trailed hungry, hot kisses along the sensitive curve of her neck. "To tell you that I didn't give a damn why you'd told your parents you were marrying me. I wanted to marry you any way I could. It was my stupid pride that made me lash out at you, Stacey, and it didn't take me long to realize that I didn't care about my pride if it meant not having you."

"My parents and I didn't mention my disastrous appearance on Cord Marshall's show, Justin. And I didn't mention marrying you, either. When I told

my Mother about the babies, she assumed that—
She and Dad started making plans. . . ."

"As well they should, sweetheart. I talked to your
mother before I drove down here. The wedding is
still on for tonight, Stacey."

"No! Oh, we *can't* get married, Justin!" She
twisted restlessly beneath him.

"Stacey, we can't *not* get married." He silenced
her with a long, slow kiss. Stacey was just a hair-
breadth away from melting completely when he
lifted his head. "We are getting married, love."

"Justin, I know you want to do the right thing,
the honorable thing, but . . ."

"I don't want to marry you because I'm honorable
or dutiful, Stacey. I want to marry you because I
love you. I asked you to marry me before I knew
about our babies." His face suddenly came alive
with a glowing brightness. "When Patty told me
about our twins, I was almost delirious with happiness. Having children of my own—with you as
their mother—seemed like the realization of a
golden dream." He shifted his weight so that he lay
alongside her, although he still kept her arms
anchored above her head, his fingers interwoven
with hers. "Then I realized that you hadn't been
able to tell me yourself that you were going to have
my baby—babies. I'd made myself totally unapproachable to you. And Stacey, it hurt like hell. I
want you to feel so close to me, so confident of me
that you can tell me anything."

"It wasn't just you, Justin," she said softly, aching at the unhappiness in his dark, dark eyes. "It
was partly me too. I was confused and guilty
and"—her lips quirked into a wry smile—"more
than a little cowardly."

He released one of her hands and touched his
fingertips to her lips, lightly tracing the shape of
her mouth. "Stacey, I don't blame you for not want-

ing to marry that political automaton who heads your father's staff. I've thought and thought about what happened to us on Friday, when we were both in the office. We'd been inseparable for two wonderful days, yet the moment I was back in my role as campaign manager and administrative aide, everything started to come apart with us. That's why I resigned from both positions this morning, Stacey. As of ten A.M., I'm no longer in politics."

"What?" She tried to sit up, but he held her down, staring into her eyes with an intensity that dizzied her. "Justin, you can't mean . . . You didn't really . . ." She broke off, staring up at him in stunned shock.

"You were right, you know." He cupped her cheek with his big hand, his eyes serious. "We couldn't have made it work as things were. I would be too involved and absorbed with the campaign and you would be miserable in a political marriage that you never wanted. And I don't want an unhappy wife, Stacey. I've waited too long for a home and family of my own to settle for anything less than a strong, solid marriage. We're getting married, Stacey, and it's going to work. We're going to make it last."

His fierceness shook her. She'd seen that iron determination achieve remarkable results in the past ten years. Justin Marks never failed at anything he set out to do. "But to resign . . ." she breathed. "Justin, I can't ask that of you!"

"You didn't," he said quietly. "I decided that it had to be done and I did it. I love you, Stacey, I've loved you for years. I'm not going to risk losing you and my children. Your happiness is my number-one priority."

"But what about *your* happiness?" she cried. She could hardly take it all in. How could Justin quit a job that had been his whole life? He was a proud and ambitious man gifted with incredible energy and talent. "You can't leave politics, Justin! You live and breathe it. You love it!"

He shrugged. "I love you more. Having you in my apartment those few days gave me a glimpse of what real happiness is. Caring for someone, sharing a home, loving and laughing together. Building a life with you, Stacey, loving you and making you happy—that's happiness for me."

"But, Justin, what will you do? You're a brilliant man, you *need* to work."

"Don't worry, honey, you're not going to be saddled with an unemployed husband." He smiled and her heart turned over. It seemed as if it had been ages since she'd last seen him smile. "I mentioned to you that I'd once been interested in teaching economics on the university level. I was sidetracked first by the world of marketing in New York and then by the Washington political scene, but I retained contact with the academic world. More importantly, I've met many influential people in the field over the years. After I resigned from your father's staff this morning, I made a few phone calls. Would you like to live in Cambridge, Massachusetts, Stacey? I've been offered a position on the faculty of the Harvard Business School, to begin with the summer session in June. We'll have a lot of time to spend together—alone—before the babies are born."

"You're really serious, aren't you?" Stacey was crying now. She seemed to be doing little else lately. "Oh, Justin, I can't let you do it. You're giving up everything for me and it isn't fair! What if Dad wins the nomination, and then the election? I don't want you to come to resent me—to hate me!—because you're not a part of it all."

"Will you marry me if I stay on with your father's staff? Will you live in Washington and keep the home fires burning while I'm involved in the campaign twenty-six hours a day? Will you raise our children alone while I'm devoting all my time and efforts to my political career, Stacey?"

"Yes!" She broke free from his hold and threw her arms around his neck. "Oh, yes, Justin, because I love you and I want *you* to be happy!"

"Stacey." He hugged her tightly, then kissed her with a lingering tenderness. "You've made me very happy, love, because I know what it cost you to say that. And I think it's very noble and sweet and generous of you, but I'm not going to accept your offer." He held her close and stroked her hair with gentle hands. "I've waited thirty-nine years for a home and family of my own and I intend to be fully involved in my wife's and children's lives. Politics won't allow me to have the kind of marriage I want to have or be the kind of father I want to be. So . . . as far as I'm concerned, my political career is history."

Stacey stared at him with loving awe. "You gave up coffee in the same way. The all-or-nothing approach. Justin, I can't let you sacrifice—"

"It's no sacrifice, Stacey," he interrupted softly. "I've always had the good sense to know what's good for me and I've never been afraid to risk change to get it. And look what I'm getting—a wife, two babies, a home, a new and interesting job with great hours." His ebony eyes gleamed. "A job where I can wear sweaters and loafers instead of gray suits and black wing-tips."

She clung to him. "Oh, Justin, are you sure?"

"I've never been surer of anything in my entire life."

Her arms tightened possessively around him. "Justin, my father was very upset when you told him you were leaving, wasn't he?" She could envision the scene and she shivered.

"Honey, there are any number of eager young men with as much or more political ambition, cunning, and instincts as I have. Several of them are already on the staff and the senator will have no trouble attracting more. I'm certainly not irreplaceable."

"But you are," she whispered. He wasn't going to tell her what had transpired in her father's office that morning. He wanted to protect her, to spare her the unpleasantness. "Oh, Justin, you're irreplaceable to me!"

"Will you marry me, Stacey? Tonight? And then we'll go away for a while, just the two of us."

"Yes." She gazed up at him, the love shining in her golden-brown eyes. "Yes to everything, Justin." She joyfully accepted, buoyed by his own confident optimism. "Oh, Justin, we're going to be so happy together. We'll have the most wonderful marriage and the most wonderful home and the most wonderful babies. . . ."

Their bodies intertwined and, kissing passionately, they sank down into the warm, sweet-smelling hay.

Epilogue

The delegation from the state of Wisconsin announced that it was proud to give Senator Bradford Lipton the votes he needed to secure the presidential nomination. Pandemonium broke loose in the huge convention center as the Lipton delegates cheered and whistled, blew horns and danced around to celebrate their candidate's victory. The network anchorman informed the viewers that the senator and his wife were watching the proceedings on TV in their hotel suite and would make an appearance in the convention hall within the hour.

In the living room of their comfortable Cambridge house, Stacey and Justin Marks were also watching the convention on television. Justin was holding Amanda, who sucked solemnly on her pacifier, while Stacey cuddled Allison, who dozed through all the excitement. The identical twin girls had been born in a Boston hospital three months earlier.

"This is an important night for you, Mandy," Justin said to the infant, who watched him intently, as if trying hard to interpret his words. "A little baby doesn't often see her grandfather win the presidential nomination, you know."

Amanda's big dark eyes began to close. Justin

chuckled. "She's certainly taking it in stride. And Allie is even less impressed."

Stacey glanced from the television screen to her husband and smiled at the sight of the drowsy infant in his big hands. Justin had been fully involved with his daughters from the moment of their birth. He had even been the first to hold them in the delivery room. His teaching schedule permitted him to spend evenings and weekends and even part of the day with his family.

They were incredibly happy, yet as Stacey watched the excitement on TV where, as the newscaster proclaimed, "History was being made," she couldn't help but wonder if Justin felt a pang or a qualm about his decision to leave politics.

"Justin, now that Dad's won the nomination, are you just a little bit sorry that you're here and the team is . . . there celebrating the victory?"

"I've been expecting that question from you all night." Justin shifted little Amanda to his left arm and gathered Stacey close to him with his right. "And I'll answer it honestly, Stacey."

She gazed up at him seriously.

"No, I'm not the least bit sorry, sweetheart. When I make a decision, I never look back. And I wouldn't trade what we have together for the lunacy of a presidential campaign, even if I knew that victory was assured in November."

Stacey leaned against him, her head on his shoulder. "That's what I thought you would say, but I guess I just wanted to hear the words.

"Oh, look!" She sat up suddenly and leaned forward to peer at the television screen. "The cameras are on the family box, Justin! There's Brynn—I'm so glad that Mom invited her along. And there's Sterne and Spence and Patty and the kids!"

"Why are the children wearing bathing suits?" Justin wondered aloud. "And what on earth are they eating? And *who* is that chesty blonde in the high heels and short-shorts and halter top who's hanging all over Sterne?"

"All of America will soon be asking those questions." Stacey laughed. "Poor Freddie Rhodes! As his predecessor, can you guess what he's feeling, Justin?"

"I wouldn't trade places with him for all the world!" was Justin's heartfelt reply.

"I wonder why Senator Lipton's grandchidren are wearing bathing suits?" the network anchorman mused over the air. "And I'm curious as to the . . . unusual food they're eating."

"I'm curious as to the identity of Sterne Lipton's companion," the co-anchor chimed in dryly. Sterne and the blonde were avidly necking, oblivious to their millions of onlookers.

Justin and Stacey looked at each other and laughed. They cuddled close on the sofa, their babies in their arms, and waited for the senator and his wife to appear on the screen.

THE EDITOR'S CORNER

We have four festive, touching LOVESWEPTs to complement the varied aspects of the glorious holiday season coming up.

First, remember what romance and fun you found in Joan Bramsch's **THE LIGHT SIDE** (LOVESWEPT #81)? And, especially, do you remember Sky's best friend and house mate, that magnificent model, Hooker Jablonski? Well, great news! Joan has given Hooker his very own love story ... **THE STALLION MAN**, LOVESWEPT #119. And for her modern day Romeo, Hooker, Joan has provided the perfect heroine in Juliet McLane. Juliet's a music teacher and musician ... and a "most practical lady." And it certainly isn't practical for a woman to fall for her fantasy lover! Hooker must teach the teacher a few lessons about the difference between image and reality ... and that he most definitely is flesh-and-blood reality! You'll relish this warm romance from talented Joan Bramsch.

How many times I've told you in our Editor's Corner about our great pleasure in finding and presenting a brand new romance writer. That is such a genuine sentiment shared by all of us at LOVESWEPT. So it is with much delight that we publish next month Hertha Schulze's first love story, **BEFORE AND AFTER**, LOVESWEPT #120. And what a debut book this is! Heroine Libby Carstairs is a little pudgy, a little dowdy, and a heck of a brainy Ph.D. student. Hero Blake Faulkner is a very worldly, very successful fashion photographer, and one heck of a man! He makes a reckless wager with a pompous make-up artist that he can turn Libby into a cover girl in just a few short weeks. Mildly insulted, but intrigued, Libby goes along with the bet ... then she begins to fall for the devastating Blake and the gambol turns serious. We think you're going to adore this thoroughly charming and chuckle-filled Pygmalion-type romance! And what a nifty, heartwarming twist it takes at the end!

TEMPEST, LOVESWEPT #121, marks the return to our list of the much loved Helen Mittermeyer. With her characteristic verve and storytelling force Helen gives us

(continued)

the passionate love story of Sage and Ross Tempest, whose love affair throughout their marriage has been stormy (which may even be putting it mildly). And, as always, you can count on Helen to enhance her romance with the endearing elements, as well as the downright funny ones that make her such a popular author. You'll long remember little Pip and Tad, not just Sage and Ross . . . and one very special, very naughty turkey!

A SUMMER SMILE, LOVESWEPT #122, by Iris Johansen is guaranteed to warm your heart and soul no matter how blustery the day is next month when you read it. Iris brings together two of her wonderfully memorable characters for their own bold, exciting love story. Daniel Seifert—remember Beau's captain in **BLUE VELVET**?— is given a hair-raising assignment to rescue a young woman from terrorists. She is Zilah, whom David took under his wing (**TOUCH THE HORIZON**) and helped to heal. Sparks fly—literally and figuratively— between this unlikely couple as they flee through the desert to safety in Sedikhan. Yet, learning Zilah's tragic secret, Daniel is frozen with fear . . . fear that only **A SUMMER SMILE** can melt. Oh, what a romantic reading experience this is!

All of us at LOVESWEPT wish you the happiest of holiday seasons.

Sincerely,

Carolyn Nichols

Carolyn Nichols
  Editor
LOVESWEPT
Bantam Books, Inc.
666 Fifth Avenue
New York, NY 10103

P.S. In case you forgot to send in your questionnaire last month, we're running it again on the next page. We'd really appreciate it if you could take the time and trouble to fill it out and return it to us.

Dear Reader:

As you know, our goal is to give you a "keeper" with every love story we publish. In our view a "keeper" blends the traditional beloved elements of a romance with truly original ingredients of characterization or plot or setting. Breaking new ground can be risky, but it's well worth it when one succeeds. We hope we succeed almost all the time. Now, well on the road to our third anniversary, we would appreciate a progress report from you. Please take a moment to let us know how you think we're doing.

1. Overall the quality of our stories has *improved* ☐
                                     declined ☐
                          remained the same ☐

2. Would you trust us to increase the number of books we publish each month without sacrificing quality?   *yes* ☐   *no* ☐

3. How many romances do you buy each month? _____

4. Which romance brands do you regularly read?

_____

_____

_____

_____

_____

_____

           I choose my books by author, not brand name ☐

5. Please list your three favorite authors from other lines:

6. Please list your six favorite LOVESWEPT authors:

7. Would you be interested in buying reprinted editions of your favorite LOVESWEPT authors' romances published in the early months of the line?

8. Is there a special message you have for us? (Attach a page, if necessary.)

With our thanks to you for taking the time and trouble to respond,

Sincerely,

Carolyn Nichols

Valentina—she's a beauty, an enigma, a warm, sensitive woman, a screen idol . . . goddess.

GODDESS

By Margaret Pemberton

There was a sound of laughter, of glasses clinking. A sense of excitement so deep it nearly took her breath away, seized her. With glowing eyes Valentina stepped into the noise and heat of the party.

"Lilli wants to meet you," a girl with a friendly smile said, grabbing hold of Valentina's hand and tugging her into the throng. "I'm Patsy Smythe. Have you met Lilli before?"

"No," Daisy said, avoiding the appreciative touch of a strange male hand.

Patsy grinned. "Just treat her as if she's the Queen of Sheba and you won't go far wrong.

Oh, someone has spilled rum on my skirt. How do you get rum stains out of chiffon?"

Valentina didn't know. Her gaze met Lilli Rainer's. Lilli's eyes were small and piercing, raisin-black in a powdered white face. She had been talking volubly, a long jade cigarette holder stabbing the air to emphasize her remarks. Now she halted, her anecdote forgotten. She had lived and breathed for the camera. Only talkies had defeated her. Her voice held the guttural tones of her native Germany and no amount of elocution lessons had been able to eradicate them. She had retired gracefully, allowing nobody to know of her bitter frustration. On seeing Valentina, she rose imperiously to her feet. No star or starlet from Worldwide Studios had been invited to the party. She did not like to be outshone and the girl before her, with her effortless grace and dark, fathom-deep eyes was doing just that. Everyone had turned in her direction as Patsy Smythe had led her across the room.

Lilli's carmine-painted lips tightened. "This is not a studio party," she said icily. "Admittance is by invitation only."

Valentina smiled. "I've been invited," she said pleasantly. "I came with Bob Kelly."

Lilli sat down slowly and gestured away those surrounding them. The amethyst satin dress Valentina wore was pathetically cheap and yet it looked marvelous on the girl. A spasm of jealousy caught at her aged throat and was gone. It was only the second rate that she could not tolerate. And the girl in front of her was far from second rate. "Do you work at Worldwide?" she asked sharply.

"No."

"Then you ought to," Lilli said tersely, "It's a first-rate studio and it has one of the best directors in town." She drew on her cigarette, inhaling deeply. "Where is Bob going to take you? Warner Brothers? Universal?"

"Not to any one of them," Valentina said composedly, not allowing her inner emotions to show. "Bob doesn't want me to work at the studios."

Lilli blew a wreath of smoke into the air and stared at her. "Then he's a fool," she said tartly. "You belong in front of the cameras. Anyone with half an eye can see that."

Noise rose and ebbed about them. Neither of them heard it.

"I know," Valentina said sharply and with breathtaking candor. "But Bob doesn't. Not yet."

Lilli crushed her cigarette out viciously. "And how long are you going to wait until he wakes up to reality? Whose life are you leading? Yours or his?" She leaned forward, grasping hold of Valentina's wrist, her eyes brilliant.

"There are very few, my child, a very tiny few, who can be instantly beloved by the cameras. It's nothing that can be learned. It's something you are born with. It's in here . . ." She stabbed at her head with a lacquered fingernail, "and in here . . ." She slapped her hand across her corseted stomach. "It's *inside* you. It's not actions and gestures, it's something that is innate." She released Valentina's wrist and leaned back in her chair. "And you have it."

Valentina could feel her heart beating in short, sharp strokes. Lilli was telling her what she already knew, and it was almost more than she could bear.

She had to get away. She needed peace and quiet in order to be able to think clearly. To still the unsettling emotions Lilli's words had aroused.

She fought her way from the crowded room into the ornate entrance hall. A chandelier hung brilliantly above her head; the carpet was wine-red, the walls covered in silk. There was a marble telephone stand and a dark, carved wooden chair beside it. She sat down, her legs trembling as if she were on the edge of an abyss. Someone had left cigarettes and a lighter on the telephone table. Clumsily she spilled them from their pack, picking one up, struggling with the lighter.

"Allow me," a deep-timbred voice said from the shadows of the stairs. The lighter clattered to the table, the cigarette dropped from her fingers as she whirled her head round.

He had been sitting on the stairs, just out of range of the chandelier's brilliance. Now he moved, rising to his feet, walking toward her with the athletic ease and sexual negligence of a natural born predator.

She couldn't speak, couldn't move. He withdrew a black Sobrainie from a gold cigarette case, lit it, inhaling deeply and then removed the cigarette from his mouth and set it gently between her lips.

She was shaking. Over the abyss and falling. Falling as Vidal Rakoczi softly murmured her name.

Goddess

* * *

There was still noise. Laughter and music were still loud in nearby rooms but Valentina was oblivious to it. She was aware of nothing but the dark, magnetic face staring down at her, the eyes pinning her in place, consuming her like dry tinder in a forest fire. She tried to stand, to gather some semblance of dignity, but could do neither. The wine-red of the walls and carpet, the brilliance of the chandelier, all spun around her in a dizzy vortex of light and color and in the center, drawing her like a moth to a flame, were the burning eyes of Vidal Rakoczi. She was suffocating, unable to breathe, to draw air into her lungs. The cigarette fell from her lips, scorching the amethyst satin. Swiftly he swept it from her knees, crushing it beneath his foot.

"Are you hurt?" The depth of feeling in his voice shocked her into mobility.

"I . . . No . . ." Unsteadily she rose to her feet. He made no movement to stand aside, to allow her to pass.

He was so close that she could feel the warmth of his breath on her cheek, smell the indefinable aroma of his maleness.

"Will you excuse me?" she asked, a pulse beating wildly in her throat.

"No." The gravity in his voice held her transfixed. His eyes had narrowed. They were bold and black and blatantly determined. "Now that I have found you again, I shall never excuse you to leave me. Not ever."

She felt herself sway and his hand grasped her arm, steadying her.

"Let's go where we can talk."

"No," she whispered, suddenly terrified as her dreams took on reality. She tried to pull away from him but he held her easily.

"Why not?" A black brow rose questioningly.

The touch of his hand seared her flesh. She could not go with him. To go with him would be to abandon Bob and that was unthinkable. He had done nothing to deserve such disloyalty. He had been kind to her. Kinder than anyone else had ever been. Sobs choked her throat. She loved Bob, but not in the way that he needed her to love him. The day would have come when she would have had to tell him so . . . but it hadn't come, and she couldn't just leave with Rakoczi. Not like this.

"No," she said again, her lips dry, her mouth parched. "Please let me go."

The strong, olive-toned hand tightened on her arm and the earth seemed to tremble beneath her feet. It was as if the very foundations upon which she had built her life since leaving the convent were cracking and crumbling around her. She made one last, valiant attempt to cling to the world that had been her haven.

"I came with Bob Kelly," she said, knowing even as she spoke that her battle was lost. "He will be looking for me."

A slight smile curved the corners of his mouth. "But he won't find you," he said. With devastating assurance he took her hand, and the course of her life changed.

Goddess

She wasn't aware of leaving the house. She wasn't aware of anything but Vidal Rakoczi's hand tightly imprisoning hers as she ran to keep up with his swift stride.

She sat in silence at his side in his car, peace and contentment lost to her forever. Something long dormant had at last been released. A zest, a recklessness for life that caused the blood to pound along her veins, and her nerve ends to throb. Like had met like. She had known it instinctively the day he had stalked across to her on the studio lot. Now there was no going back. No acceptance of anything less than life with the man who was at her side.

The car crowned a dune and he braked and halted. In the moonlight the heaving Pacific was silk-black, the swelling waves breaking into surging foam on a crescent of firm white sand. The night breeze from the sea was salt-laden and chilly. He took off his dinner jacket and draped it around her shoulders as they slipped and slid down the dunes to the beach. She stepped out of her high-heeled sandals, raising her face to the breeze.

"It's very beautiful here. And very lonely."

"That's why I come."

They walked down along in silence for a while, the Pacific breakers creaming and running up the shoreline only inches from their feet.

"You know what it is I want of you, don't you?" he asked at last, and a shiver ran down her spine. Whatever it was, she would give it freely. "I want to film you. To see if the luminous quality you posess transfers to the screen."

The moon slid out from behind a bank of clouds. He had expected lavish thanks; vows of eternal gratitude; a silly stream of nonsense about how she had always wanted to be a movie star. Instead she remained silent, her face strangely serene. There was an inner stillness to her that he found profoundly refreshing. He picked up a pebble and skimmed it far out into the night-black sea.

"I am a man of instincts," he said, stating a fact that no one who had come into contact with him would deny. "I believe that you have a rare gift, Valentina." Their hands touched fleetingly and she trembled. "I expect complete obedience. Absolute discipline."

His brows were pulled close together, his silhouetted face that of a Roman emperor accustomed to wielding total power. He halted, staring down at her. "Do you understand?"

Her head barely reached his shoulder. She turned her face up to his, the sea-breeze fanning her hair softly against her cheeks. The moonlight accentuated the breath-taking purity of her cheekbone and jaw line.

"Yes," she said, and at her composure his eyes gleamed with amusement.

"Where the devil did you spring from?" he asked, a smile touching his mouth.

Her eyes sparkled in the darkness as she said with steely determination. "Wherever it was, I'm not going back."

He began to laugh and as he did so she stumbled, falling against him. His arms closed around her, steadying her. For a second they remained motionless and then the laughter faded from his eyes and he lowered his head, his mouth claiming hers in swift, sure contact.

Nothing had prepared her for Vidal's kiss. Her lips trembled and then parted willingly beneath his. There was sudden shock and an onrush of pleasure as his tongue sought and demanded hers, setting her on fire.

 # LOVESWEPT

Love Stories you'll never forget by authors you'll always remember

Prices and availability subject to change without notice.

Buy them at your local bookstore or use this handy coupon for ordering:

Bantam Books, Inc., Dept. SW, 414 East Golf Road, Des Plaines, Ill. 60016

Please send me the books I have checked above. I am enclosing $_____ (please add $1.25 to cover postage and handling). Send check or money order —no cash or C.O.D.'s please.

Mr/Mrs/Miss_____

Address_____

City_____State/Zip_____

SW—10/85

Please allow four to six weeks for delivery. This offer expires 4/86.

LOVESWEPT

Love Stories you'll never forget by authors you'll always remember

LOVESWEPT

Love Stories you'll never forget by authors you'll always remember

Prices and availability subject to change without notice.

Buy them at your local bookstore or use this handy coupon for ordering:

Bantam Books, Inc., Dept. SW3, 414 East Golf Road, Des Plaines, Ill. 60016

Please send me the books I have checked above. I am enclosing $_____
(please add $1.25 to cover postage and handling). Send check or money order
—no cash or C.O.D.'s please.

Mr/Mrs/Miss _____

Address _____

City _____ State/Zip _____

SW3—12/85

Please allow four to six weeks for delivery. This offer expires 6/86.

LOVESWEPT

Love Stories you'll never forget by authors you'll always remember